Ron Gaultier

The Book of Ballads

Edited by Bon Gaultier and Illustrated by Doyle, Leech, and Crowguill

Ron Gaultier

The Book of Ballads
Edited by Bon Gaultier and Illustrated by Doyle, Leech, and Crowguill

ISBN/EAN: 9783744779425

Printed in Europe, USA, Canada, Australia, Japan

Cover: Foto ©Andreas Hilbeck / pixelio.de

More available books at **www.hansebooks.com**

The

Book of Ballads

EDITED BY

Bon Gaultier

AND ILLUSTRATED BY

Doyle, Leech, and Crowquill

Eighth Edition

WILLIAM BLACKWOOD AND SONS

EDINBURGH AND LONDON

MDCCCLXIV

CONTENTS.

Spanish Ballads.

American Ballads.

Miscellaneous Ballads.

L'ENVOY.

Come, buy my lays, and read them if you list:
My pensive public, if you list not, buy.
Come, for you know me.   I am he who sung
Of Mister Colt, and I am he who framed
Of Widdicomb the wild and wondrous song.

L'ENVOY.

Come, listen to my lays, and you shall hear
How Wordsworth, battling for the Laureate's wreath,
Bore to the dust the terrible Fitzball;
How N. P. Willis for his country's good,
In complete steel, all bowie-knifed at point,
Took lodgings in the Snapping Turtle's womb.
Come, listen to my lays, and you shall hear
The mingled music of all modern bards
Floating aloft in such peculiar strains,
As strike themselves with envy and amaze;
For you "bright-harped" Tennyson shall sing:
Macaulay chant a more than Roman lay;
And Bulwer Lytton, Lytton Bulwer erst,
Unseen amidst a metaphysic fog,
Howl melancholy homage to the moon:
For you once more Montgomery shall rave
In all his rapt rapidity of rhyme;
Nankeened Cockaigne shall pipe his puny note,
And our young England's penny trumpet blow.

Spanish Ballads

The Broken Pitcher.

IT was a Moorish maiden was sitting by a well,
And what the maiden thought of, I cannot, cannot tell,
When by there rode a valiant knight from the town of
　　Oviedo —
Alphonzo Guzman was he hight, the Count of Tololedo.

"Oh, maiden, Moorish maiden, why sitt'st thou by the
　　spring?
Say, dost thou seek a lover, or any other thing?
Why dost thou look upon me, with eyes so dark and wide,
And wherefore doth the pitcher lie broken by thy side?"

" I do not seek a lover, thou Christian knight so gay,
Because an article like that hath never come my way :
And why I gaze upon you, I cannot, cannot tell,
Except that in your iron hose you look uncommon swell.

" My pitcher it is broken, and this the reason is,—
A shepherd came behind me, and tried to snatch a kiss ;
I would not stand his nonsense, so ne'er a word I spoke,
But scored him on the costard, and so the jug was broke.

" My uncle, the Alcaydé, he waits for me at home,
And will not take his tumbler until Zorayda come :
I cannot bring him water—the pitcher is in pieces—
And so I'm sure to catch it, 'cos he wallops all his nieces."

" Oh, maiden, Moorish maiden ! wilt thou be ruled by me !
So wipe thine eyes and rosy lips, and give me kisses three ;
And I'll give thee my helmet, thou kind and courteous lady,
To carry home the water to thy uncle, the Alcaydé."

He lighted down from off his steed—he tied him to a
        tree—
He bent him to the maiden, and he took his kisses three ;
"To wrong thee, sweet Zorayda, I swear would be a sin !"
And he knelt him at the fountain, and he dipped his
        helmet in.

Up rose the Moorish maiden—behind the knight she steals,
And caught Alphonzo Guzman in a twinkling by the heels :
She tipped him in, and held him down beneath the bubbling
    water.—
" Now, take thou that for venturing to kiss Al Hamet's
    daughter ! "

A Christian maid is weeping in the town of Oviedo ;
She waits the coming of her love, the Count of Tololedo.
I pray you all in charity, that you will never tell,
How he met the Moorish maiden beside the lonely well.

Don Fernando Gomersalez.

Don Fernando Gomersalez! basely have
they borne thee down;
Paces ten behind thy charger is thy
glorious body thrown;
Fetters have they bound upon thee—iron
fetters, fast and sure;
Don Fernando Gomersalez, thou art cap-
tive to the Moor!

Long within a dingy dungeon pined that brave and noble
knight,
For the Saracenic warriors well they knew and feared his
might ;
Long he lay and long he languished on his dripping bed
of stone,
Till the cankered iron fetters ate their way into his bone.

On the twentieth day of August—'twas the feast of false
Mahound—
Came the Moorish population from the neighbouring cities
round ;
There to hold their foul carousal, there to dance and there
to sing,
And to pay their yearly homage to Al-Widdicomb, the
King !

First they wheeled their supple coursers, wheeled them at
their utmost speed,
Then they galloped by in squadrons, tossing far the light
jereed ;
Then around the circus racing, faster than the swallow
flies,
Did they spurn the yellow sawdust in the rapt spectator's
eyes.

Proudly did the Moorish monarch every passing warrior
    greet,
As he sate enthroned above them, with the lamps beneath
    his feet :
" Tell me, thou black-bearded Cadi ! are there any in the
    land,
That against my janissaries dare one hour in combat stand ?"

Then the bearded Cadi answered—" Be not wroth, my lord,
    the King,
If thy faithful slave shall venture to observe one little thing ;

Valiant, doubtless, are thy warriors, and their beards are
    long and hairy,
And a thunderbolt in battle is each bristly janissary :

" But I cannot, O my sovereign, quite forget that fearful
    day,
When I saw the Christian army in its terrible array ;
When they charged across the footlights like a torrent
    down its bed,
With the red cross floating o'er them, and Fernando at
    their head !

" Don Fernando Gomersalez ! matchless chieftain he in war,
Mightier than Don Sticknejo, braver than the Cid Bivar !
Not a cheek within Grenada, O my King, but wan and
    pale is,
When they hear the dreaded name of Don Fernando
    Gomersalez !"

" Thou shalt see thy champion, Cadi ! hither quick the
    captive bring !"
Thus in wrath and deadly anger spoke Al-Widdicomb, the
    King :
" Paler than a maiden's forehead is the Christian's hue, I
    ween,
Since a year within the dungeons of Grenada he hath
    been !"

Then they brought the Gomersalez, and they led the
     warrior in ;
Weak and wasted seemed his body, and his face was pale
     and thin ;
But the ancient fire was burning, unallayed, within his eye,
And his step was proud and stately, and his look was stern
     and high.

Scarcely from tumultuous cheering could the galleried
     crowd refrain,
For they knew Don Gomersalez and his prowess in the
     plain ;
But they feared the grizzly despot and his myrmidons in
     steel,
So their sympathy descended in the fruitage of Seville.

" Wherefore, monarch, hast thou brought me from the
     dungeon dark and drear,
Where these limbs of mine have wasted in confinement
     for a year ?
Dost thou lead me forth to torture ?—Rack and pincers
     I defy !
Is it that thy base grotesquos may behold a hero die ?"

" Hold thy peace, thou Christian caitiff, and attend to what
     I say :
Thou art called the starkest rider of the Spanish cur's array :

If thy courage be undaunted, as they say it was of yore,
Thou may'st yet achieve thy freedom,—yet regain thy
native shore.

" Courses three within this circus 'gainst my warriors shalt
thou run,
Ere yon weltering pasteboard ocean shall receive yon
muslin sun ;
Victor—thou shalt have thy freedom ; but if stretched
upon the plain,
To thy dark and dreary dungeon they shall hale thee back
again."

" Give me but the armour, monarch, I have worn in many
a field,
Give me but my trusty helmet, give me but my dinted
shield ;
And my old steed, Bavieca, swiftest courser in the ring.
And I rather should imagine that I'll do the business, King!"

Then they carried down the armour from the garret where
it lay,
O ! but it was red and rusty, and the plumes were shorn
away :
And they led out Bavieca from a foul and filthy van,
For the conqueror had sold him to a Moorish dogs'-meat
man.

When the steed beheld his master, then he whinnied loud
　　　and free,
And in token of subjection, knelt upon each broken knee:
And a tear of walnut largeness to the warrior's eyelids
　　　rose,
As he fondly picked a bean-straw from his coughing
　　　courser's nose.

" Many a time, O Bavieca, hast thou borne me through
　　　the fray :
Bear me but again as deftly through the listed ring this
　　　day ;
Or if thou art worn and feeble, as may well have come to
　　　pass,
Time it is, my trusty charger, both of us were sent to grass !"

Then he seized his lance, and vaulting in the saddle sate
　　　upright ;
Marble seemed the noble courser, iron seemed the mailèd
　　　knight ;
And a cry of admiration burst from every Moorish lady—
" Five to four on Don Fernando !" cried the sable-bearded
　　　Cadi.

Warriors three from Alcantara burst into the listed space,
Warriors three, all bred in battle, of the proud Alhambra
　　　race :

Trumpets sounded, coursers bounded, and the foremost
    straight went down,
Tumbling, like a sack of turnips, just before the jeering
    Clown.

In the second chieftain galloped, and he bowed him to the
    King,
And his saddle-girths were tightened by the Master of the
    Ring;
Through three blazing hoops he bounded ere the desperate
    fight began—
Don Fernando! bear thee bravely!—'tis the Moor Abdor-
    rhoman!

Like a double streak of lightning, clashing in the sulphurous
    sky,
Met the pair of hostile heroes, and they made the sawdust
    fly;
And the Moslem spear so stiffly smote on Don Fernando's
    mail,
That he reeled, as if in liquor, back to Bavieca's tail:

But he caught the mace beside him, and he griped it hard
    and fast,
And he swung it starkly upwards as the foeman bounded
    past;

And the deadly stroke descended through the skull and
  through the brain.
As ye may have seen a poker cleave a cocoa-nut in twain.

Sore astonished was the monarch, and the Moorish warriors
  all.
Save the third bold chief, who tarried and beheld his
  brethren fall :
And the Clown, in haste arising from the footstool where
  he sat,
Notified the first appearance of the famous Acrobat ;

Never on a single charger rides that stout and stalwart
  Moor,—
Five beneath his stride so stately bear him o'er the
  trembling floor ;
Five Arabians, black as midnight—on their necks the rein
  he throws,
And the outer and the inner feel the pressure of his toes.

Never wore that chieftain armour ; in a knot himself he
  ties,
With his grizzly head appearing in the centre of his
  thighs,
Till the petrified spectator asks, in paralysed alarm,
Where may be the warrior's body,—which is leg, and
  which is arm ?

"Sound the charge!"   The coursers started; with a yell
    and furious vault,
High in air the Moorish champion cut a wondrous somer-
    sault;
O'er the head of Don Fernando like a tennis-ball he sprung,
Caught him tightly by the girdle, and behind the crupper
    hung.

Then his dagger Don Fernando plucked from out its
    jewelled sheath,
And he struck the Moor so fiercely, as he grappled him
    beneath,

That the good Damascus weapon sunk within the folds of
　　fat.
And as dead as Julius Cæsar dropped the Gordian
　　Acrobat.

Meanwhile fast the sun was sinking—it had sunk beneath
　　the sea,
Ere Fernando Gomersalez smote the latter of the three ;
And Al-Widdicomb, the monarch, pointed, with a bitter
　　smile,
To the deeply-darkening canvass ;—blacker grew it all the
　　while.

" Thou hast slain my warriors, Spaniard ! but thou hast
　　not kept thy time ;
Only two had sunk before thee ere I heard the curfew
　　chime ;
Back thou goest to thy dungeon, and thou may'st be
　　wondrous glad
That thy head is on thy shoulders for thy work to-day,
　　my lad !

" Therefore all thy boasted valour, Christian dog, of no
　　avail is !"
Dark as midnight grew the brow of Don Fernando Gomer-
　　salez ;—

Stilly sate he in his saddle, grimly looked around the
    ring,
Laid his lance within the rest, and shook his gauntlet at
    ˙ the King.

"O, thou foul and faithless traitor! wouldst thou play me
    false again?
Welcome death and welcome torture, rather than the
    captive's chain!
But I give thee warning, caitiff! Look thou sharply to
    thine eye—
Unavenged, at least in harness, Gomersalez shall not
    die!"

Thus he spoke, and Bavieca like an arrow forward flew,
Right and left the Moorish squadron wheeled to let the
    hero through;
Brightly gleamed the lance of vengeance—fiercely sped
    the fatal thrust—
From his throne the Moorish monarch tumbled lifeless in
    the dust.

Speed thee, speed thee, Bavieca! speed thee faster than
    the wind!
Life and freedom are before thee, deadly foes give chase
    behind!

Speed thee up the sloping spring-board : o'er the bridge
    that spans the seas ;
Yonder hazy moon will light thee through the grove of
    hazel trees.

Close before thee, Pampeluna spreads her painted pasteboard gate !
Speed thee onward, gallant courser, speed thee with thy
knightly freight !
Victory ! The town receives them !—Gentle ladies, this
the tale is,
Which I learned in Astley's Circus, of Fernando Gomersalez.

The Courtship of our Cid.

WHAT a pang of sweet emotion
   Thrilled the Master of the Ring,
When he first beheld the lady
   Through the stabled portal spring !
Midway in his wild grimacing
   Stopped the piebald-visaged Clown ;
And the thunders of the audience
   Nearly brought the gallery down.

Donna Inez Woolfordinez !
    Saw ye ever such a maid,
With the feathers swaling o'er her,
    And her spangled rich brocade ?
In her fairy hand a horsewhip,
    On her foot a buskin small,
So she stepped, the stately damsel,
    Through the scarlet grooms and all.

And she beckoned for her courser,
    And they brought a milk-white mare ;
Proud, I ween, was that Arabian
    Such a gentle freight to bear :
And the Master moved to greet her,
    With a proud and stately walk ;
And, in reverential homage,
    Rubbed her soles with virgin chalk.

Round she flew, as Flora flying
    Spans the circle of the year ;
And the youth of London, sighing,
    Half forgot the ginger-beer—
Quite forgot the maids beside them ;
    As they surely well might do,
When she raised two Roman candles,
    Shooting fireballs red and blue !

Swifter than the Tartar's arrow,
  Lighter than the lark in flight,
On the left foot now she bounded,
  Now she stood upon the right.
Like a beautiful Bacchante,
  Here she soars, and there she kneels,
While amid her floating tresses
  Flash two whirling Catherine wheels !

Hark ! the blare of yonder trumpet !
  See, the gates are opened wide !
Room, there, room for Gomersalez,—
  Gomersalez in his pride !
Rose the shouts of exultation,
  Rose the cat's triumphant call,
As he bounded, man and courser,
  Over Master, Clown, and all !

Donna Inez Woolfordinez !
  Why those blushes on thy cheek ?
Doth thy trembling bosom tell thee,
  He hath come thy love to seek ?
Fleet thy Arab, but behind thee
  He is rushing like a gale ;
One foot on his coal-black's shoulders,
  And the other on his tail !

Onward, onward, panting maiden !
  He is faint, and fails, for now
By the feet he hangs suspended
  From his glistening saddle-bow.
Down are gone both cap and feather,
  Lance and gonfalon are down !
Trunks, and cloak, and vest of velvet,
  He has flung them to the Clown.

Faint and failing !   Up he vaulteth,
  Fresh as when he first began ;
All in coat of bright vermilion,
  'Quipped as Shaw, the Lifeguardsman ;
Right and left his whizzing broadsword,
  Like a sturdy flail, he throws ;
Cutting out a path unto thee
  Through imaginary foes.

Woolfordinez ! speed thee onward !
  He is hard upon thy track,—
Paralysed is Widdicombez,
  Nor his whip can longer crack ;
He has flung away his broadsword,
  'Tis to clasp thee to his breast.
Onward !—see, he bares his bosom,
  Tears away his scarlet vest ;

Leaps from out his nether garments,
  And his leathern stock unties—
As the flower of London's dustmen,
  Now in swift pursuit he flies.
Nimbly now he cuts and shuffles,
  O'er the buckle, heel and toe!
Flaps his hands in his tail-pockets,
  Winks to all the throng below!

Onward, onward rush the coursers:
  Woolfordinez, peerless girl,
O'er the garters lightly bounding
  From her steed with airy whirl!
Gomersalez, wild with passion,
  Danger—all but her—forgets;
Wheresoe'er she flies, pursues her,
  Casting clouds of somersets!

Onward, onward rush the coursers:
  Bright is Gomersalez' eye;
Saints protect thee, Woolfordinez,
  For his triumph sure is nigh:
Now his courser's flanks he lashes,
  O'er his shoulder flings the rein,
And his feet aloft he tosses,
  Holding stoutly by the mane!

Then, his feet once more regaining.
   Doffs his jacket, doffs his smalls,
And in graceful folds around him
   A bespangled tunic falls.
Pinions from his heels are bursting,
   His bright locks have pinions o'er them :
And the public see with rapture
   Maia's nimble son before them.

Speed thee, speed thee, Woolfordinez !
   For a panting god pursues ;
And the chalk is very nearly
   Rubbed from thy white satin shoes ;
Every bosom throbs with terror,
   You might hear a pin to drop :
All is hushed, save where a starting
   Cork gives out a casual pop.

One smart lash across his courser.
   One tremendous bound and stride.
And our noble Cid was standing
   By his Woolfordinez' side !
With a god's embrace he clasped her,
   Raised her in his manly arms :
And the stables' closing barriers
   Hid his valour, and her charms !

American Ballads

The
Fight with the Snapping Turtle:

OR, THE AMERICAN ST GEORGE.

FYTTE FIRST.

Have you heard of Philip Slingsby,
　　Slingsby of the manly chest ;
How he slew the Snapping Turtle
　　In the regions of the West ?

Every day the huge Cawana
　　Lifted up its monstrous jaws ;
And it swallowed Langton Bennett,
　　And digested Rufus Dawes.

Riled, I ween, was Philip Slingsby,
    Their untimely deaths to hear :
For one author owed him money,
    And the other loved him dear.

" Listen now, sagacious Tyler,
    Whom the loafers all obey;
What reward will Congress give me,
    If I take this pest away?"

Then sagacious Tyler answered,
    " You're the ring-tailed squealer !   Less
Than a hundred heavy dollars
    Won't be offered you, I guess !

" And a lot of wooden nutmegs
    In the bargain, too, we'll throw—
Only you just fix the critter.
    Won't you liquor ere you go ?"

Straightway leaped the valiant Slingsby
    Into armour of Seville,
With a strong Arkansas toothpick
    Screwed in every joint of steel.

" Come thou with me, Cullen Bryant.
    Come with me, as squire, I pray ;
Be the Homer of the battle,
    Which I go to wage to-day."

So they went along careering
   With a loud and martial tramp,
Till they neared the Snapping Turtle
   In the dreary Swindle Swamp.

But when Slingsby saw the water,
   Somewhat pale, I ween, was he.
" If I come not back, dear Bryant,
   Tell the tale to Melanie !

"Tell her that I died devoted,
   Victim to a noble task !
Han't you got a drop of brandy
   In the bottom of your flask ?"

As he spoke, an alligator
   Swam across the sullen creek ;
And the two Columbians started,
   When they heard the monster shriek ;

For a snout of huge dimensions
   Rose above the waters high,
And took down the alligator,
   As a trout takes down a fly.

" 'Tarnal death ! the Snapping Turtle !"
   Thus the squire in terror cried ;
But the noble Slingsby straightway
   Drew the toothpick from his side.

" Fare thee well ! " he cried, and dashing
    Through the waters, strongly swam :
Meanwhile Cullen Bryant, watching,
    Breathed a prayer and sucked a dram.

Sudden from the slimy bottom
    Was the snout again upreared,
With a snap as loud as thunder,—
    And the Slingsby disappeared.

Like a mighty steam-ship foundering,
    Down the monstrous vision sank ;
And the ripple, slowly rolling,
    Plashed and played upon the bank.

Still and stiller grew the water,
    Hushed the canes within the brake ;
There was but a kind of coughing
    At the bottom of the lake.

Bryant wept as loud and deeply
    As a father for a son—
" He's a finished 'coon, is Slingsby,
    And the brandy's nearly done ! "

FYTTE SECOND.

In a trance of sickening anguish,
  Cold and stiff, and sore and damp,
For two days did Bryant linger
  By the dreary Swindle Swamp :

Always peering at the water,
  Always waiting for the hour
When those monstrous jaws should open
  As he saw them ope before.

Still in vain ;—the alligators
  Scrambled through the marshy brake,
And the vampire leeches gaily
  Sucked the garfish in the lake.

But the Snapping Turtle never
  Rose for food or rose for rest,
Since he lodged the steel deposit
  In the bottom of his chest.

Only always from the bottom
  Sounds of frequent coughing rolled,
Just as if the huge Cawana
  Had a most confounded cold.

—

On the bank lay Cullen Bryant,
  As the second moon arose,
Gouging on the sloping greensward
  Some imaginary foes :

When the swamp began to tremble,
  And the canes to rustle fast,
As though some stupendous body
  Through their roots were crushing past :

And the waters boiled and bubbled,
  And, in groups of twos and threes,
Several alligators bounded,
  Smart as squirrels, up the trees.

Then a hideous head was lifted,
  With such huge distended jaws,
That they might have held Goliath
  Quite as well as Rufus Dawes.

Paws of elephantine thickness
  Dragged its body from the bay,
And it glared at Cullen Bryant
  In a most unpleasant way.

Then it writhed as if in torture,
  And it staggered to and fro :
And its very shell was shaken
  In the anguish of its throe :

And its cough grew loud and louder,
　　And its sob more husky thick !
For, indeed, it was apparent
　　That the beast was very sick.

Till, at last, a spasmy vomit
    Shook its carcass through and through,
And as if from out a cannon,
    All in armour Slingsby flew.

Bent and bloody was the bowie
    Which he held within his grasp ;
And he seemed so much exhausted,
    That he scarce had strength to gasp—

"Gouge him, Bryant ! darn ye, gouge him !
    Gouge him while he's on the shore !"
Bryant's thumbs were straightway buried
    Where no thumbs had pierced before.

Right from out their bony sockets
    Did he scoop the monstrous balls ;
And, with one convulsive shudder,
    Dead the Snapping Turtle falls !

"Post the tin, sagacious Tyler !"
    But the old experienced file,
Leering first at Clay and Webster,
    Answered with a quiet smile—

" Since you dragged the 'tarnal crittur
  From the bottom of the ponds,
Here's the hundred dollars due you,
  All in Pennsylvanian Bonds!"

The Lay of Mr Colt.

[The story of Mr Colt, of which our Lay contains merely the sequel, is this:
A New York painter, of the name of Adams, had the effrontery to call upon
him one day for payment of an account, which the independent Colt settled by
cutting his creditor's head to fragments with an axe. He then packed his
body in a box, sprinkling it with salt, and despatched it to a packet bound for
New Orleans. Suspicions having been excited, he was seized, and tried before
Judge Kent. The trial is, perhaps, the most disgraceful upon the records of
any country. The ruffian's mistress was produced in court, and examined, in
disgusting detail, as to her connection with Colt, and his movements during the
days and nights succeeding the murder. The head of the murdered man was
handed to and from the court, handed up to the jury, and commented on by
witnesses and counsel; and to crown the horrors of the whole proceeding, the
wretch's own counsel, a Mr Emmet, commencing the defence with a cool
admission that his client took the life of Adams, and following it up by a detail of the whole circumstances of this most brutal murder in the first person,
as though he himself had been the murderer, ended by telling the jury, that
his client was "entitled to the sympathy of a jury of his country," as "a young
man just entering upon life, whose prospects, probably, have been permanently
blasted." Colt was found guilty; but a variety of exceptions were taken to the
charge by the judge, and after a long series of appeals, which occupied more
than a year from the date of conviction, the sentence of death was ratified by
Governor Seward. The rest of Colt's story is told in our ballad.]

STREAK THE FIRST.

* * * *

AND now the sacred rite was done, and the marriage-knot
    was tied,
And Colt withdrew his blushing wife a little way aside;
"Let's go," he said, "into my cell; let's go alone, my dear;
I fain would shelter that sweet face from the sheriff's
    odious leer.

The jailer and the hangman, they are waiting both for
      me,—
I cannot bear to see them wink so knowingly at thee !
Oh, how I loved thee, dearest !   They say that I am
      wild,
That a mother dares not trust me with the weasand of
      her child ;
They say my bowie-knife is keen to sliver into halves
The carcass of my enemy, as butchers slay their calves.
They say that I am stern of mood, because, like salted
      beef,
I packed my quartered foeman up, and marked him 'prime
      tariff ;'
Because I thought to palm him on the simple-souled John
      Bull,
And clear a small percentage on the sale at Liverpool ;
It may be so, I do not know—these things, perhaps,
      may be ;
But surely I have always been a gentleman to thee !
Then come, my love, into my cell, short bridal space is
      ours,—
Nay, sheriff, never look thy watch—I guess there's good
      two hours.
We'll shut the prison doors and keep the gaping world at
      bay,
For love is long as 'tarnity, though I must die to-day !"

STREAK THE SECOND.

The clock is ticking onward,
 It nears the hour of doom,
And no one yet hath entered
 Into that ghastly room.
The jailer and the sheriff,
 They are walking to and fro :
And the hangman sits upon the steps,
 And smokes his pipe below.
In grisly expectation
 The prison all is bound,
And, save expectoration,
 You cannot hear a sound.
The turnkey stands and ponders,—
 His hand upon the bolt,—
" In twenty minutes more, I guess.
 'Twill all be up with Colt !"
But see, the door is opened !
 Forth comes the weeping bride :
The courteous sheriff lifts his hat,
 And saunters to her side,—
"I beg your pardon, Mrs C.,
 But is your husband ready !"

" I guess you'd better ask himself,"
    Replied the woeful lady.

The clock is ticking onward,
    The minutes almost run,
The hangman's pipe is nearly out,
    'Tis on the stroke of one.
At every grated window
    Unshaven faces glare ;
There's Puke, the judge of Tennessee,
    And Lynch, of Delaware ;
And Batter, with the long black beard,
    Whom Hartford's maids know well;
And Winkinson, from Fish Kill Reach,
    The pride of New Rochelle ;
Elkanah Nutts, from Tarry Town,
    The gallant gouging boy ;
And 'coon-faced Bushwhack, from the hills
    That frown o'er modern Troy ;
Young Julep, whom our Willis loves,
    Because, 'tis said, that he
One morning from a bookstall filched
    The tale of " Melanie ;"
And Skunk, who fought his country's fight
    Beneath the stripes and stars, —
All thronging at the windows stood,
    And gazed between the bars.

The little boys that stood behind
      (Young thievish imps were they!)
Displayed considerable *nous*
      On that eventful day ;
For bits of broken looking-glass
      They held aslant on high,
And there a mirrored gallows-tree
      Met their delighted eye.*

The clock is ticking onward ;
      Hark ! hark ! it striketh one !
Each felon draws a whistling breath,
      " Time's up with Colt! he's done !"

The sheriff looks his watch again,
      Then puts it in his fob,
And turns him to the hangman,—
      " Get ready for the job. "
The jailer knocketh loudly,
      The turnkey draws the bolt,
And pleasantly the sheriff says,
      " We're waiting, Mister Colt !"

No answer ! No ! no answer !
      All's still as death within ;
The sheriff eyes the jailer,
      The jailer strokes his chin.

* A fact.

" I shouldn't wonder, Nahum, if
    It were as you suppose."
The hangman looked unhappy, and
    The turnkey blew his nose.

They entered.   On his pallet
    The noble convict lay,—
The bridegroom on his marriage-bed,
    But not in trim array.
His red right hand a razor held,
    Fresh sharpened from the hone,
And his ivory neck was severed,
    And gashed into the bone.

And when the lamp is lighted
    In the long November days,
And lads and lasses mingle
    At the shucking of the maize ;
When pies of smoking pumpkin
    Upon the table stand,
And bowls of black molasses
    Go round from hand to hand ;
When slap-jacks, maple-sugared,
    Are hissing in the pan,
And cider, with a dash of gin,
    Foams in the social can ;

When the goodman wets his whistle,
    And the goodwife scolds the child :
And the girls exclaim convulsively,
    " Have done, or I'll be riled !"
When the loafer sitting next them
    Attempts a sly caress,
And whispers, "Oh ! you 'possum,
    You've fixed my heart, I guess !"
With laughter and with weeping,
    Then shall they tell the tale,
How Colt his foeman quartered,
    And died within the jail.

The Death of Jabez Dollar.

[Before the following poem, which originally appeared in 'Fraser's Magazine,' could have reached America, intelligence was received in this country of an affray in Congress, very nearly the counterpart of that which the Author has here imagined in jest. It was very clear, to any one who observed the state of public manners in America, that such occurrences *must* happen, sooner or later. The Americans apparently felt the force of the satire, as the poem was widely reprinted throughout the States. It subsequently returned to this country, embodied in an American work on American manners, where it characteristically appeared as the writer's *own* production; and it afterwards went the round of British newspapers, as an amusing satire, by an American, of his countrymen's foibles!]

THE Congress met, the day was wet, Van Buren took the
    chair;
On either side, the statesman pride of far Kentuck was
    there.
With moody frown, there sat Calhoun, and slowly in his
    cheek
His quid he thrust, and slaked the dust, as Webster rose
    to speak.

Upon that day, near gifted Clay, a youthful member sat,
And like a free American upon the floor he spat;
Then turning round to Clay, he said, and wiped his manly
    chin,
"What kind of Locofoco's that, as wears the painter's
    skin?"

"Young man," quoth Clay, "avoid the way of Slick of
    Tennessee;
Of gougers fierce, the eyes that pierce, the fiercest gouger
    he:
He chews and spits, as there he sits, and whittles at the
    chairs,
And in his hand, for deadly strife, a bowie-knife he
    bears.

"Avoid that knife.   In frequent strife its blade, so long
    and thin,
Has found itself a resting-place his rival's ribs within."
But coward fear came never near young Jabez Dollar's
    heart,—
"Were he an alligator, I would rile him pretty smart!"

Then up he rose, and cleared his nose, and looked toward
    the chair;
He saw the stately stripes and stars,—our country's flag
    was there!
His heart beat high, with eldritch cry upon the floor he
    sprang,
Then raised his wrist, and shook his fist, and spoke his
    first harangue.

" Who sold the nutmegs made of wood—the clocks that
       wouldn't figure?
Who grinned the bark off gum-trees dark—the everlasting
       nigger?
For twenty cents, ye Congress gents, through 'tarnity I'll
       kick
That man, I guess, though nothing less than 'coon-faced
       Colonel Slick!"

The colonel smiled—with frenzy wild,—his very beard
       waxed blue,—
His shirt it could not hold him, so wrathy riled he grew;
He foams and frets, his knife he whets upon his seat
       below—
He sharpens it on either side, and whittles at his toe,—

" Oh! waken snakes, and walk your chalks!" he cried,
       with ire elate;
"Darn my old mother, but I will in wild cats whip my
       weight!
Oh! 'tarnal death, I'll spoil your breath, young Dollar, and
       your chaffing,—
Look to your ribs, for here is that will tickle them without
       laughing!"

His knife he raised—with fury crazed, he sprang across
    the hall :
He cut a caper in the air—he stood before them all :
He never stopped to look or think if he the deed should
    do,
But spinning sent the President, and on young Dollar
    flew.

They met—they closed—they sunk—they rose,—in vain
    young Dollar strove—
For, like a streak of lightning greased, the infuriate colonel
    drove
His bowie-blade deep in his side, and to the ground they
    rolled,
And, drenched in gore, wheeled o'er and o'er, locked in
    each other's hold.

With fury dumb—with nail and thumb—they struggled
    and they thrust,—
The blood ran red from Dollar's side, like rain, upon the
    dust ;
He nerved his might for one last spring, and as he sunk
    and died,
Reft of an eye, his enemy fell groaning by his side.

Thus did he 'fall within the hall of Congress, that brave
    youth ;

The bowie-knife has quenched his life of valour and of
    truth ;

And still among the statesmen throng at Washington they
    tell

How nobly Dollar gouged his man—how gallantly he fell !

The Alabama Duel.

"Young chaps, give ear, the case is clear.   You, Silas
        Fixings, you
Pay Mister Nehemiah Dodge them dollars as you're due.
You are a bloody cheat,—you are.   But spite of all your
        tricks, it
Is not in you Judge Lynch to do.   No! nohow you can
        fix it!"

Thus spake Judge Lynch, as there he sat in Alabama's
    forum,
Around he gazed, with legs upraised upon the bench before
    him ;
And, as he gave this sentence stern to him who stood
    beneath,
Still with his gleaming bowie-knife he slowly picked his
    teeth.

It was high noon, the month was June, and sultry was the
    air,
A cool gin-sling stood by his hand, his coat hung o'er his
    chair ;
All naked were his manly arms, and shaded by his hat,
Like an old senator of Rome that simple Archon sat.

" A bloody cheat ?—Oh, legs and feet !" in wrath young
    Silas cried ;
And springing high into the air, he jerked his quid
    aside.—
" No man shall put my dander up, or with my feelings
    trifle,
As long as Silas Fixings wears a bowie-knife and rifle."

" If your shoes pinch," replied Judge Lynch, " you'll very
soon have ease :
I'll give you satisfaction, squire, in any way you please :
What are your weapons ?—knife or gun ?—at both I'm
pretty spry :"
" Oh ! 'tarnal death, you're spry, you are ?" quoth Silas,
" so am I !"

Hard by the town a forest stands, dark with the shades
of time,
And they have sought that forest dark at morning's early
prime :
Lynch, backed by Nehemiah Dodge, and Silas with a
friend,
And half the town in glee came down to see that contest's
end.

They led their men two miles apart, they measured out
the ground ;
A belt of that vast wood it was, they notched the trees
around ;
Into the tangled brake they turned them off, and neither
knew
Where he should seek his wagered foe, how get him into
view.

With stealthy tread,
and stooping head, from tree
to tree they passed.
They crept beneath the crackling furze, they
held their rifles fast :
Hour passed on hour, the noonday sun
smote fiercely down, but yet
No sound to the expectant crowd proclaimed
that they had met.

And now the sun was going down, when,
hark ! a rifle's crack !
Hush—hush ! another strikes the air,—and
all their breath draw back,—
Then crashing on through bush and briar,
the crowd from either side
Rush in to see whose rifle sure with blood
the moss has dyed.

Weary with watching up and down, brave Lynch con-
ceived a plan,
An artful dodge whereby to take at unawares his man;
He hung his hat upon a bush, and hid himself hard by;
Young Silas thought he had him fast, and at the hat let
fly.

It fell; up sprung young Silas,—he hurled his gun
away;
Lynch fixed him with his rifle, from the ambush where he
lay.
The bullet pierced his manly breast—yet, valiant to the
last,
Young Fixings drew his bowie-knife, and up his foxtail*
cast.

With tottering step and glazing eye he cleared the space
between,
And stabbed the air as stabs in grim Macbeth the younger
Kean:
Brave Lynch received him with a bang that stretched him
on the ground,
Then sat himself serenely down till all the crowd drew
round.

* The Yankee substitute for the *chapeau de ene*

They hailed him with triumphant cheers—in him each
    loafer saw
The bearing bold that could uphold the majesty of law ;
And, raising him aloft, they bore him homewards at his
    ease,—
That noble judge, whose daring hand enforced his own
    decrees.

They buried Silas Fixings in the hollow where he fell,
And gum-trees wave above his grave—that tree he loved
    so well ;
And the 'coons sit chattering o'er him when the nights are
    long and damp ;
But he sleeps well in that lonely dell, the Dreary 'Possum
    Swamp.

The American's Apostrophe to Boz.

[Rapidly as oblivion does its work nowadays, the burst of amiable indignation with which enlightened America received the issue of Boz's 'Notes' can scarcely yet be forgotten. Not content with waging a universal rivalry in the piracy of the work, Columbia showered upon its author the riches of its own choice vocabulary of abuse; while some of her more fiery spirits threw out playful hints as to the propriety of gouging the "stranger," and furnishing him with a permanent suit of tar and feathers, in the very improbable event of his paying them a second visit. The perusal of these animated expressions of free opinion suggested the following lines, which those who remember Boz's book, and the festivities with which he was all but hunted to death, will at once understand. We hope we have done justice to the bitterness and "immortal hate" of these thin-skinned sons of freedom. When will Americans cease to justify the ridicule of Europe, by bearing rebuke, or even misrepresentation, calmly as a great nation should?]

SNEAK across the wide Atlantic, worthless London's puling
    child.
Better that its waves should bear thee, than the land thou
    hast reviled:
Better in the stifling cabin, on the sofa thou shouldst lie,
Sickening as the fetid nigger bears the greens and bacon by;
Better, when the midnight horrors haunt the strained and
    creaking ship,
Thou shouldst yell in vain for brandy with a fever-sodden
    lip:
When amid the deepening darkness and the lamp's ex-
    piring shade,

From the bagman's berth above thee comes the bountiful
    cascade.
Better than upon the Broadway thou shouldst be at noon-
    day seen,
Smirking like a Tracy Tupman with a Mantalini mien,
With a rivulet of satin falling o'er thy puny chest,
Worse than even N. P. Willis for an evening party drest !

We received thee warmly—kindly—though we knew thou
    wert a quiz,
Partly for thyself it may be, chiefly for the sake of Phiz !
Much we bore, and much we suffered, listening to remorse-
    less spells
Of that Smike's unceasing drivellings, and these everlast-
    ing Nells.
When you talked of babes and sunshine, fields, and all
    that sort of thing,
Each Columbian inly chuckled, as he slowly sucked his
    sling ;
And though all our sleeves were bursting, from the many
    hundreds near
Not one single scornful titter rose on thy complacent ear.
Then to show thee to the ladies, with our usual want of sense
We engaged the place in Park Street at a ruinous expense :
Even our own three-volumed Cooper waived his old pre-
    scriptive right.
And deluded Dickens figured first on that eventful night.

Clusters of uncoated Yorkers, vainly striving to be cool,
Saw thee desperately plunging through the perils of La
    Poule :
And their muttered exclamation drowned the tenor of the
    tune,—
"Don't he beat all natur hollow ?   Don't he foot it like a
    'coon ?"

Did we spare our brandy-cocktails, stint thee of our whisky-
    grogs ?
Half the juleps that we gave thee would have floored a
    Newman Noggs ;
And thou took'st them in so kindly, little was there then
    to blame,
To thy parched and panting palate sweet as mother's milk
    they came.
Did the hams of old Virginny find no favour in thine
    eyes ?
Came no soft compunction o'er thee at the thought of
    pumpkin pies ?
Could not all our chicken fixings into silence fix thy scorn ?
Did not all our cakes rebuke thee, Johnny, waffle, dander,
    corn ?
Could not all our care and coddling teach thee how to draw
    it mild ?
Well, no matter, we deserve it.   Serves us right !   We
    spoilt the child !

You, forsooth, must come crusading, boring us with broad-
    est hints
Of your own peculiar losses by American reprints.
Such an impudent remonstrance never in our face was flung :
Lever stands it, so does Ainsworth ; *you*, I guess, may hold
    your tongue.
Down our throats you'd cram your projects, thick and hard
    as pickled salmon,
That, I s'pose, you call free trading,—I pronounce it utter
    gammon.
No, my lad, a 'cuter vision than your own might soon
    have seen
That a true Columbian ogle carries little that is green ;
That we never will surrender useful privateering rights,
Stoutly won at glorious Bunker's Hill, and other famous
    fights ;
That we keep our native dollars for our native scribbling
    gents,
And on British manufacture only waste our straggling cents :
Quite enough we pay, I reckon, when we stump of these a few
For the voyages and travels of a freshman such as you.

I have been at Niagara, I have stood beneath the Falls,
I have marked the water twisting over its rampagious walls ;
But "a holy calm sensation," one, in fact, of perfect peace,
Was as much my first idea as the thought of Christmas
    geese.

As for "old familiar faces," looking through the misty air.
Surely you were strongly liquored when you saw your
          Chuckster there.
One familiar face, however, you will very likely see,
If you'll only treat the natives to a call in Tennessee,
Of a certain individual, true Columbian every inch,
In a high judicial station, called by 'mancipators, Lynch.
Half an hour of conversation with his worship in a wood,
Would, I strongly notion, do you an infernal deal of good.
Then you'd understand more clearly than you ever did
          before,
Why an independent patriot freely spits upon the floor,
Why he gouges when he pleases, why he whittles at the
          chairs,
Why for swift and deadly combat still the bowie-knife he
          bears,—
Why he sneers at the old country with republican disdain.
And, unheedful of the negro's cry, still tighter draws his
          chain.
All these things the judge shall teach thee of the land thou
          hast reviled ;
Get thee o'er the wide Atlantic, worthless London's puling
          child !

Miscellaneous Ballads

The Student of Jena.

Once—'twas when I lived at Jena—
　　At a Wirthshaus' door I sat ;
And in pensive contemplation
　　Ate the sausage thick and fat :
Ate the kraut, that never sourer
　　Tasted to my lips than here ;
Smoked my pipe of strong canaster
　　Sipped my fifteenth jug of beer ;
Gazed upon the glancing river,
　　Gazed upon the tranquil pool.

Whence the silver-voiced Undine,
　　When the nights were calm and cool,
As the Baron Fouqué tells us,
　　Rose from out her shelly grot,
Casting glamour o'er the waters,
　　Witching that enchanted spot.
From the shadow which the coppice
　　Flings across the rippling stream,
Did I hear a sound of music—
　　Was it thought or was it dream?
There, beside a pile of linen,
　　Stretched along the daisied sward,
Stood a young and blooming maiden—
　　'Twas her thrush-like song I heard.
Evermore within the eddy
　　Did she plunge the white chemise;
And her robes were loosely gathered
　　Rather far above her knees;
Then my breath at once forsook me,
　　For too surely did I deem
That I saw the fair Undine
　　Standing in the glancing stream—
And I felt the charm of knighthood:
　　And from that remembered day,
Every evening to the Wirthshaus
　　Took I my enchanted way.

Shortly to relate my story,
   Many a week of summer long,
Came I there, when beer-o'ertaken,
   With my lute and with my song:
Sung in mellow-toned soprano
   All my love and all my woe,
Till the river-maiden answered,
   Lilting in the stream below :—
" Fair Undine ! sweet Undine !
   Dost thou love as I love thee !"
" Love is free as running water,"
   Was the answer made to me.

Thus, in interchange seraphic,
   Did I woo my phantom fay,
Till the nights grew long and chilly,
   Short and shorter grew the day:
Till at last—'twas dark and gloomy,
   Dull and starless was the sky,
And my steps were all unsteady,
   For a little flushed was I,—
To the well-accustomed signal
   No response the maiden gave :
But I heard the waters washing,
   And the moaning of the wave.

Vanished was my own Undine,
   All her linen, too, was gone ;
And I walked about lamenting
   On the river bank alone.
Idiot that I was, for never
   Had I asked the maiden's name.
Was it Lieschen—was it Gretchen ?
   Had she tin, or whence she came ?
So I took my trusty meerschaum,
   And I took my lute likewise ;
Wandered forth in minstrel fashion,
   Underneath the lowering skies ;
Sang before each comely Wirthshaus,
   Sang beside each purling stream,
That same ditty which I chanted
   When Undine was my theme,
Singing, as I sang at Jena,
   When the shifts were hung to dry,
" Fair Undine ! young Undine !
   Dost thou love as well as I ?"

But, alas ! in field or village,
   Or beside the pebbly shore,
Did I see those glancing ankles,
   And the white robe never more :

And no answer came to greet me,
    No sweet voice to mine replied;
But I heard the waters rippling,
    And the moaning of the tide.

" The meaning of the tide."

The Lay of the Levite.

THERE is a sound that's dear to me,
　It haunts me in my sleep:
I wake, and, if I hear it not,
　I cannot choose but weep.
Above the roaring of the wind,
　Above the river's flow,
Methinks I hear the mystic cry
　Of "Clo!—Old Clo!"

The exile's song, it thrills among
　The dwellings of the free,

Its sound is strange to English ears,
    But 'tis not strange to me ;
For it hath shook the tented field
    In ages long ago,
And hosts have quailed before the cry
    Of "Clo !—Old Clo !"

Oh, lose it not ! forsake it not !
    And let no time efface
The memory of that solemn sound,
    The watchword of our race ;
For not by dark and eagle eye
    The Hebrew shall you know,
So well as by the plaintive cry
    Of "Clo !—Old Clo !"

Even now, perchance, by Jordan's banks,
    Or Sidon's sunny walls,
Where, dial-like, to portion time,
    The palm-tree's shadow falls,
The pilgrims, wending on their way,
    Will linger as they go,
And listen to the distant cry
    Of "Clo !—Old Clo !"

Bursch Groggenburg.

[. . . .]

"Burschen! if foaming beer content ye,
    Come and drink your fill;
In our cellars there is plenty;
    Himmel! how you swill!
That the liquor hath allurance,
    Well I understand;
But 'tis really past endurance,
    When you squeeze my hand!"

And he heard her as if dreaming,
    Heard her half in awe:

And the meerschaum's smoke came streaming
   From his open jaw :
And his pulse beat somewhat quicker
   Than it did before,
And he finished off his liquor,
   Staggered through the door ;

Bolted off direct to Munich,
   And within the year
Underneath his German tunic
   Stowed whole butts of beer.
And he drank like fifty fishes,
   Drank till all was blue ;
For he felt extremely vicious—
   Somewhat thirsty too.

But at length this dire deboshing
   Drew towards an end ;
Few of all his silber-groschen
   Had he left to spend.
And he knew it was not prudent
   Longer to remain ;
So, with weary feet, the student
   Wended home again.

At the tavern's well-known portal
   Knocks he as before,

And a waiter, rather mortal,
    Hiccups through the door,—
" Master's sleeping in the kitchen :
    You'll alarm the house :
Yesterday the Jungfrau Fritchen
    Married baker Kraus !"

Like a fiery comet bristling,
    Rose the young man's hair,
And, poor soul ! he fell a-whistling
    Out of sheer despair.
Down the gloomy street in silence,
    Savage-calm he goes ;
But he did no deed of vi'lence—
    Only blew his nose.

Then he hired an airy garret
    Near her dwelling-place ;
Grew a beard of fiercest carrot,
    Never washed his face ;
Sate all day beside the casement,
    Sate a dreary man ;
Found in smoking such an easement
    As the wretched can ;

Stared for hours and hours together,
    Stared yet more and more ;

Till in fine and sunny weather,
    At the baker's door,
Stood, in apron white and mealy,
    That belovèd dame,
Counting out the loaves so freely,
    Selling of the same.

Then like a volcano puffing,
    Smoked he out his pipe ;
Sighed and supped on ducks and stuffing,
    Ham and kraut and tripe ;
Went to bed, and, in the morning,
    Waited as before,
Still his eyes in anguish turning
    To the baker's door ;

Till, with apron white and mealy,
    Came the lovely dame,
Counting out the loaves so freely,
    Selling of the same.
So one day—the fact's amazing !—
    On his post he died !
And they found the body gazing
    At the baker's bride.

Night and Morning.

[Parody on E. Bulwer Lytton.]

"Thy coffee, Tom, 's untasted,
    And thy egg is very cold;
Thy cheeks are wan and wasted,
    Not rosy as of old.
My boy, what has come o'er ye?
    You surely are not well!
Try some of that ham before ye,
    And then, Tom, ring the bell!"

"I cannot eat, my mother,
    My tongue is parched and bound,
And my head, somehow or other,
    Is swimming round and round.
In my eyes there is a fulness,
    And my pulse is beating quick;
On my brain is a weight of dulness;
    Oh, mother, I am sick!"

" These long, long nights of watching
    Are killing you outright ;
The evening dews are catching,
    And you're out every night.
Why does that horrid grumbler,
    Old Inkpen, work you so ? "

               (Tom—*lene susurrans*)

" My head ! Oh, that tenth tumbler !
    'Twas that which wrought my woe ! "

The Biter Bit.

THE sun is in the sky, mother, the flowers are springing
    fair.
And the melody of woodland birds is stirring in the air;
The river, smiling to the sky, glides onward to the sea,
And happiness is everywhere, oh mother, but with me!

They are going to the church, mother,—I hear the mar-
    riage-bell;
It booms along the upland,—oh! it haunts me like a
    knell;
He leads her on his arm, mother, he cheers her faltering
    step,
And closely to his side she clings,—she does, the demirep!

They are crossing by the stile, mother, where we so oft
    have stood,
The stile beside the shady thorn, at the corner of the
    wood;
And the boughs, that wont to murmur back the words
    that won my ear,
Wave their silver blossoms o'er him, as he leads his bridal
    fere.

He will pass beside the stream, mother, where first my
　　hand he pressed,
By the meadow where, with quivering lip, his passion he
　　confessed ;
And down the hedgerows where we've strayed again and
　　yet again ;
But he will not think of me, mother, his broken-hearted
　　Jane !

He said that I was proud, mother,—that I looked for rank
　　and gold ;
He said I did not love him,—he said my words were
　　cold ;
He said I kept him off and on, in hopes of higher
　　game,—
And it may be that I did, mother ; but who hasn't done
　　the same ?

I did not know my heart, mother,—I know it now too
　　late ;
I thought that I without a pang could wed some nobler
　　mate ;
But no nobler suitor sought me,—and he has taken wing,
And my heart is gone, and I am left a lone and blighted
　　thing.

You may lay me in my bed, mother,—my head is throb-
     bing sore ;
And, mother, prithee, let the sheets be duly aired before :
And, if you'd do a kindness to your poor desponding
     child,
Draw me a pot of beer, mother, and, mother, draw it mild!

The Meeting.

Once I lay beside a fountain,
    Lulled me with its gentle song,
And my thoughts o'er dale and mountain
    With the clouds were borne along.

There I saw old castles flinging
    Shadowy gleams on moveless seas,
Saw gigantic forests swinging
    To and fro without a breeze;

And in dusky alleys straying,
    Many a giant shape of power,
Troops of nymphs in sunshine playing,
    Singing, dancing, hour on hour.

I, too, trod these plains Elysian,
    Heard their ringing tones of mirth,
But a brighter, fairer vision
    Called me back again to earth.

From the forest shade advancing,
    See, where comes a lovely May;
The dew, like gems, before her glancing,
    As she brushes it away!

Straight I rose, and ran to meet her,
　　Seized her hand—the heavenly blue
Of her eyes smiled brighter, sweeter,
　　As she asked me—" Who are you ?"

To that question came another ;
　　What its aim I still must doubt,
And she asked me, "How's your mother :
　　Does she know that you are out ?"

" No ! my mother does not know it,
　　Beauteous, heaven-descended muse !"
" Then be off, my handsome poet,
　　And say I sent you with the news !"

The Convict and the Australian Lady.

Thy skin is dark as jet, ladye,
    Thy cheek is sharp and high,
And there's a cruel leer, love,
    Within thy rolling eye :
These tangled ebon tresses
    No comb hath e'er gone through ;
And thy forehead, it is furrowed by
    The elegant tattoo !

I love thee,—oh, I love thee,
 Thou strangely-feeding maid !
Nay, lift not thus thy boomerang,
 I meant not to upbraid !
Come, let me taste those yellow lips
 That ne'er were tasted yet,
Save when the shipwrecked mariner
 Passed through them for a whet.

Nay, squeeze me not so tightly !
 For I am gaunt and thin;
There's little flesh to tempt thee
 Beneath a convict's skin.
I came not to be eaten ;
 I sought thee, love, to woo ;
Besides, bethink thee, dearest,
 Thou'st dined on cockatoo.

Thy father is a chieftain !
 Why, that's the very thing !
Within my native country
 I too have been a king.
Behold this branded letter,
 Which nothing can efface !
It is the royal emblem,
 The token of my race !

But rebels rose against me,
    And dared my power disown—
You've heard, love, of the judges !
    They drove me from my throne.
And I have wandered hither,
    Across the stormy sea,
In search of glorious freedom,—
    In search, my sweet, of thee !

The bush is now my empire,
    The knife my sceptre keen ;
Come with me to the desert wild,
    And be my dusky queen.
I cannot give thee jewels,
    I have nor sheep nor cow,
Yet there are kangaroos, love,
    And colonists enow.

We'll meet the unwary settler,
    As whistling home he goes,
And I'll take tribute from him,
    His money and his clothes.
Then on his bleeding carcass
    Thou'lt lay thy pretty paw,
And lunch upon him, roasted,
    Or, if you like it, raw !

Then come with me, my princess,
   My own Australian dear,
Within this grove of gum trees
   We'll hold our bridal cheer !
Thy heart with love is beating,
   I feel it through my side :—
Hurrah, then, for the noble pair,
   The Convict and his Bride !

The

Doleful Lay of the Honourable I. O. Uwins.

COME and listen, lords and ladies,
    To a woeful lay of mine ;
He whose tailor's bill unpaid is,
    Let him now his ear incline !
Let him hearken to my story,
    How the noblest of the land
Pined in piteous purgatory,
    'Neath a sponging Bailiff's hand.

I. O. Uwins ! I. O. Uwins !
    Baron's son although thou be,
Thou must pay for thy misdoings
    In the country of the free !
None of all thy sire's retainers
    To thy rescue now may come ;
And there lie some score detainers
    With Abednego, the bum.

Little recked he of his prison
    Whilst the sun was in the sky :
Only when the moon was risen,
    Did you hear the captive's cry.
For till then, cigars and claret
    Lulled him in oblivion sweet ;

— — ..

And he much preferred a garret,
    For his drinking, to the street.

But the moonlight, pale and broken,
    Pained at soul the Baron's son ;
For he knew, by that soft token,
    That the larking had begun ;—
That the stout and valiant Marquis
    Then was leading forth his swells,
Milling some policeman's carcass,
    Or purloining private bells.

So he sat in grief and sorrow,
    Rather drunk than otherwise,
Till the golden gush of morrow
    Dawned once more upon his eyes :
Till the sponging Bailiff's daughter,
    Lightly tapping at the door,
Brought his draught of soda-water,
    Brandy-bottomed as before.

"Sweet Rebecca! has your father,
    Think you, made a deal of brass ?"
And she answered—"Sir, I rather
    Should imagine that he has."
Uwins then, his whiskers scratching,
    Leered upon the maiden's face,

And, her hand with ardour catching,
    Folded her in close embrace.

" La, Sir ! let alone—you fright me ! "
    Said the daughter of the Jew :
" Dearest, how those eyes delight me !
    Let me love thee, darling, do ! "
" Vat is dish ? " the Bailiff muttered,
    Rushing in with fury wild ;
" Ish your muffins so vell buttered,
    Dat you darsh insult ma shild ? "

" Honourable my intentions,
    Good Abednego, I swear !
And I have some small pretensions,
    For I am a Baron's heir.
If you'll only clear my credit,
    And advance a *thou* * or so.
She's a peeress—I have said it :
    Don't you twig, Abednego ? "

" Datsh a very different matter,"
    Said the Bailiff, with a leer ;
" But you musht not cut it fatter
    Than ta slish will shtand, ma tear !
If you seeksh ma approbation,
    You musht quite give up your rigsh

---

* The fashionable abbreviation for a thousand pounds.

Alsho you musht join our nashun,
  And renounsh ta flesh of pigsh."

Fast as one of Fagin's pupils,
  I. O. Uwins did agree!
Little plagued with holy scruples
  From the starting-post was he.
But at times a baleful vision
  Rose before his shuddering view,
For he knew that circumcision
  Was expected from a Jew.

At a meeting of the Rabbis,
  Held about the Whitsuntide,
Was this thorough-paced Barabbas
  Wedded to his Hebrew bride :
All his previous debts compounded,
  From the sponging-house he came,
And his father's feelings wounded
  With reflections on the same.

But the sire his son accosted—
  "Split my wig! if any more
Such a double-dyed apostate
  Shall presume to cross my door!
Not a penny-piece to save ye
  From the kennel or the spout ;—

Dinner, John ! the pig and gravy !—
    Kick this dirty scoundrel out !"

Forth rushed I. O. Uwins, faster
    Than all winking—much afraid,
That the orders of the master
    Would be punctually obeyed :
Sought his club, and then the sentence
    Of expulsion first he saw ;
No one dared to own acquaintance
    With a Bailiff's son-in-law.

Uselessly, down Bond Street strutting,
    Did he greet his friends of yore :
Such a universal cutting
    Never man received before :
Till at last his pride revolted—
    Pale, and lean, and stern he grew ;
And his wife Rebecca bolted
    With a missionary Jew.

Ye who read this doleful ditty,
    Ask ye where is Uwins now ?
Wend your way through London city,
    Climb to Holborn's lofty brow ;
Near the sign-post of the "Nigger,"
    Near the baked-potato shed,

You may see a ghastly figure
    With three hats upon his head.

When the evening shades are dusky,
    Then the phantom form draws near,
And, with accents low and husky,
    Pours effluvium in your ear ;
Craving an immediate barter
    Of your trousers or surtout ;
And you know the Hebrew martyr,
    Once the peerless I. O. U.

The Knyghte

and the

Taylzeour's Daughter.

Did you ever hear the story--
    Old the legend is and true—
How a knyghte of fame and glory
    All aside his armour threw :
Spouted spear and pawned habergeon.
    Pledged his sword and surcoat gay,
Sate down cross-legged on the shop-board.
    Sate and stitched the livelong day ?

" Taylzeour ! not one single shilling
    Does my breeches pocket hold :
I to pay am really willing,
    If I only had the gold.
Farmers none can I encounter,
    Graziers there are none to kill ;
Therefore, prithee, gentle taylzeour,
    Bother not about thy bill."

"Good Sir Knyghte, just once too often
    Have you tried that slippery trick ;
Hearts like mine you cannot soften,
    Vainly do you ask for tick.
Christmas and its bills are coming,
    Soon will they be showering in ;
Therefore, once for all, my rum un,
    I expect you'll post the tin.

"Mark, Sir Knyghte, that gloomy bayliffe
    In the palmer's amice brown ;
He shall lead you unto jail, if
    Instantly you stump not down."
Deeply swore the young crusader,
    But the taylzeour would not hear ;
And the gloomy, bearded bayliffe
    Evermore kept sneaking near.

" Neither groat nor maravedi
    Have I got my soul to bless ;

And I'd feel extremely seedy,
    Languishing in vile duresse.
Therefore listen, ruthless taylzeour,
    Take my steed and armour free,
Pawn them at thy Hebrew uncle's,
    And I'll work the rest for thee."

Lightly leaped he on the shop-board,
    Lightly crooked his manly limb,
Lightly drove the glancing needle
    Through the growing doublet's rim.
Gaberdines in countless number
    Did the taylzeour knyghte repair,
And entirely on cucumber
    And on cabbage lived he there.

Once his weary task beguiling
    With a low and plaintive song,
That good knyghte o'er miles of broadcloth
    Drove the hissing goose along ;
From her lofty latticed window
    Looked the taylzeour's daughter down,
And she instantly discovered
    That her heart was not her own.

"Canst thou love me, gentle stranger ?"
    Picking at a pink she stood—
And the knyghte at once admitted
    That he rather thought he could.

" He who weds me shall have riches,
    Gold, and lands, and houses free."
" For a single pair of—*small-clothes*,
    I would roam the world with thee ! "

Then she flung him down the tickets—
    Well the knyghte their import knew—
" Take this gold, and win thy armour
    From the unbelieving Jew.
Though in garments mean and lowly,
    Thou wouldst roam the world with me,

Only as a belted warrior,
　　Stranger, will I wed with thee !"

At the feast of good Saint Stichem,
　　In the middle of the Spring,
There was some superior jousting
　　By the order of the King.
" Valiant knyghtes !" proclaimed the monarch.
　　" You will please to understand,
He who bears himself most bravely
　　Shall obtain my daughter's hand."

Well and bravely did they bear them,
　　Bravely battled, one and all ;
But the bravest in the tourney
　　Was a warrior stout and tall.
None could tell his name or lineage,
　　None could meet him in the field,
And a goose regardant proper
　　Hissed along his azure shield.

" Warrior, thou hast won my daughter !"
　　But the champion bowed his knee,
" Royal blood may not be wasted
　　On a simple knyghte like me.
She I love is meek and lowly ;
　　But her heart is kind and free :
Also, there is tin forthcoming,
　　Though she is of low degree."

Slowly rose that nameless warrior,
    Slowly turned his steps aside,
Passed the lattice where the princess
    Sate in beauty, sate in pride.
Passed the row of noble ladies,
    Hied him to an humbler seat,
And in silence laid the chaplet
    At the taylzeour's daughter's feet.

The Midnight Visit.

It was the Lord of Castlereagh, he sat within his room,
His arms were crossed upon his breast, his face was
     marked with gloom :
They said that St Helena's Isle had rendered up its
     charge,
That France was bristling high in arms—the Emperor at
     large.

Twas midnight! all the lamps were dim, and dull as
    death the street.
It might be that the watchman slept that night upon his
    beat,
When lo! a heavy foot was heard to creak upon the
    stair,
The door revolved upon its hinge—Great Heaven!—What
    enters there?

A little man, of stately mien, with slow and solemn
    stride :
His hands are crossed upon his back, his coat is opened
    wide ;
And on his vest of green he wears an eagle and a
    star,—
Saint George! protect us! 'tis THE MAN—the thunder-
    bolt of war!

Is that the famous hat that waved along Marengo's
    ridge?
Are these the spurs of Austerlitz—the boots of Lodi's
    bridge?
Leads he the conscript swarm again from France's hornet
    hive?
What seeks the fell usurper here, in Britain, and alive?

Pale grew the Lord of Castlereagh, his tongue was parched
    and dry,
As in his brain he felt the glare of that tremendous eye ;
What wonder if he shrunk in fear, for who could meet the
    glance
Of him who reared, 'mid Russian snows, the gonfalon of
    France ?

From the side-pocket of his vest a pinch the despot
    took,
Yet not a whit did he relax the sternness of his look :
"Thou thoughtst the lion was afar, but he hath burst the
    chain—
The watchword for to-night is France—the answer St
    Helène.

"And didst thou deem the barren isle, or ocean waves,
    could bind
The master of the universe—the monarch of mankind ?
I tell thee, fool ! the world itself is all too small for me :
I laugh to scorn thy bolts and bars—I burst them, and
    am free.

"Thou thinkst that England hates me ! Mark !—This
    very night my name
Was thundered in its capital with tumult and acclaim !

They saw me, knew me, owned my power—Proud lord!
    I say, beware!
There be men within the Surrey side, who know to do
    and dare!

"To-morrow in thy very teeth my standard will I rear—
Ay, well that ashen cheek of thine may blanch and shrink
    with fear!
To-morrow night another town shall sink in ghastly
    flames;
And as I crossed the Borodin, so shall I cross the
    Thames!

"Thou'lt seize me, wilt thou, ere the dawn? Weak
    lordling, do thy worst!
These hands ere now have broke thy chains, thy fetters
    they have burst.
Yet, wouldst thou know my resting-place? Behold, 'tis
    written there!
And let thy coward myrmidons approach me if they dare!"

Another pinch, another stride—he passes through the
    door—
"Was it a phantom or a man was standing on the floor?
And could that be the Emperor that moved before my eyes?
Ah, yes! too sure it was himself, for here the paper lies!"

With trembling hands Lord Castlereagh undid the mystic
    scroll,
With glassy eye essayed to read, for fear was on his soul—
"What's here?—'At Astley's, every night, the play of
    Moscow's FALL!
NAPOLEON, for the thousandth time, by Mr GOMERSAL.'"

The Lay of the Lovelorn.

Comrades, you may pass the rosy. With permission of
    the chair,
I shall leave you for a little, for I'd like to take the air.

Whether 'twas the sauce at dinner, or that glass of ginger-
    beer,
Or those strong cheroots, I know not, but I feel a little queer.

Let me go. Nay, Chuckster, blow me, 'pon my soul, this
    is too bad !
When you want me, ask the waiter ; he knows where I'm
    to be had.

Whew! This is a great relief now! Let me but undo my
    stock;
Resting here beneath the porch, my nerves will steady
    like a rock.

In my ears I hear the singing of a lot of favourite tunes—
Bless my heart, how very odd! Why, surely there's a
    brace of moons!

See! the stars! how bright they twinkle, winking with a
    frosty glare,
Like my faithless cousin Amy when she drove me to
    despair.

Oh, my cousin, spider-hearted! Oh, my Amy! No, con-
    found it!
I must wear the mournful willow,—all around my hat
    I've bound it.

Falser than the Bank of Fancy, frailer than a shilling glove,
Puppet to a father's anger, minion to a nabob's love!

Is it well to wish thee happy? Having known me, could
    you ever
Stoop to marry half a heart, and little more than half a
    liver?

Happy !   Damme !   Thou shalt lower to his level day by
      day,
Changing from the best of china to the commonest of
      clay.

As the husband is, the wife is,—he is stomach-plagued
      and old ;
And his curry soups will make thy cheek the colour of
      his gold.

When his feeble love is sated, he will hold thee surely
      then
Something lower than his hookah,—something less than
      his cayenne.

What is this ?   His eyes are pinky.   Was't the claret ?
      Oh, no, no,—
Bless your soul ! it was the salmon,—salmon always makes
      him so.

Take him to thy dainty chamber—soothe him with thy
      lightest fancies ;
He will understand thee, won't he ?—pay thee with a
      lover's glances ?

Louder than the loudest trumpet, harsh as harshest
    ophicleide,
Nasal respirations answer the endearments of his bride.

Sweet response, delightful music! Gaze upon thy noble
    charge,
Till the spirit fill thy bosom that inspired the meek
    Laffarge.

Better thou wert dead before me,—better, better that I
    stood,
Looking on thy murdered body, like the injured Daniel
    Good!

Better thou and I were lying, cold and timber-stiff and
    dead,
With a pan of burning charcoal underneath our nuptial
    bed!

Cursed be the Bank of England's notes, that tempt the
    soul to sin!
Cursed be the want of acres,—doubly cursed the want of tin!

Cursed be the marriage-contract, that enslaved thy soul
    to greed!
Cursed be the sallow lawyer, that prepared and drew the
    deed!

Cursed be his foul apprentice, who the loathsome fees did
    earn !
Cursed be the clerk and parson,—cursed be the whole
    concern !

Oh, 'tis well that I should bluster,—much I'm like to
    make of that ;
Better comfort have I found in singing " All Around my
    Hat."

But that song, so wildly plaintive, palls upon my British
    ears.
'Twill not do to pine for ever.—I am getting up in
    years.

Can't I turn the honest penny, scribbling for the weekly
    press,
And in writing Sunday libels drown my private wretched-
    ness ?

Oh, to feel the wild pulsation that in manhood's dawn I
    knew,
When my days were all before me, and my years were
    twenty-two !

When I smoked my independent pipe along the Quadrant
    wide,
With the many larks of London flaring up on every side :

When I went the pace so wildly, caring little what might
    come ;
Coffee-milling care and sorrow, with a nose-adapted thumb :

Felt the exquisite enjoyment, tossing nightly off, oh
    heavens !
Brandy at the Cider Cellars, kidneys smoking-hot at
    Evans' !

Or in the Adelphi sitting, half in rapture, half in tears,
Saw the glorious melodrama conjure up the shades of
    years !

Saw Jack Sheppard, noble stripling, act his wondrous feats
    again,
Snapping Newgate's bars of iron, like an infant's daisy
    chain.

Might was right, and all the terrors, which had held the
    world in awe,
Were despised, and prigging prospered, spite of Laurie,
    spite of law.

In such scenes as these I triumphed, ere my passion's
　　edge was rusted,
And my cousin's cold refusal left me very much dis-
　　gusted !

Since, my heart is sere and withered, and I do not care a
　　curse,
Whether worse shall be the better, or the better be the
　　worse.

Hark ! my merry comrades call me, bawling for another
　　jorum ;
They would mock me in derision, should I thus appear
　　before 'em.

Womankind no more shall vex me, such at least as go
　　arrayed
In the most expensive satins and the newest silk brocade.

I'll to Afric, lion-haunted, where the giant forest yields
Rarer robes and finer tissue than are sold at Spital-
　　fields.

Or to burst all chains of habit, flinging habit's self
　　aside,
I shall walk the tangled jungle in mankind's primeval
　　pride ;

Feeding on the luscious berries and the rich cassava root,
Lots of dates and lots of guavas, clusters of forbidden
fruit.

Never comes the trader thither, never o'er the purple
main
Sounds the oath of British commerce, or the accents of
Cockaigne.

There, methinks, would be enjoyment, where no envious
rule prevents :
Sink the steamboats ! cuss the railways ! rot, O rot the
Three per Cents !

There the passions, cramped no longer, shall have space
to breathe, my cousin !
I will wed some savage woman—nay, I'll wed at least a
dozen.

There I'll rear my young mulattoes, as no Bond Street
brats are reared :
They shall dive for alligators, catch the wild goats by the
beard—

Whistle to the cockatoos, and mock the hairy-faced
baboon,
Worship mighty Mumbo Jumbo in the Mountains of the
Moon.

I myself, in far Timbuctoo, leopard's blood will daily
quaff,
Ride a tiger-hunting, mounted on a thorough-bred giraffe.

Fiercely shall I shout the war-whoop, as some sullen
stream he crosses,
Startling from their noonday slumbers iron-bound rhino-
ceroses.

Fool! again the dream, the fancy! But I know my words
are mad,
For I hold the grey barbarian lower than the Christian
cad.

I the swell—the city dandy! I to seek such horrid
places,—
I to haunt with squalid negroes, blubber-lips, and monkey-
faces.

I to wed with Coromantees! I, who managed—very
near—
To secure the heart and fortune of the widow Shilli-
beer!

Stuff and nonsense! let me never fling a single chance
away:
Maids are now, I know, have loved me, and another
maiden may.

' Morning Post' ('The Times' won't trust me),
    help me, as I know you can ;
I will pen an advertisement,—that's a never-
    failing plan.

" WANTED—By a bard in wedlock, some young
    interesting woman :
Looks are not so much an object, if the shiners
    be forthcoming !

" Hymen's chains the advertiser vows shall be
    but silken fetters;
Please address to A. T., Chelsea.   N.B.—You
    must pay the letters."

That's the sort of thing to do it.   Now I'll go
    and taste the balmy,—
Rest thee with thy yellow nabob, spider-hearted
    Cousin Amy !

My Wife's Cousin.

DE KED with shoes of blackest polish,
   And with shirt as white as snow,
After matutinal breakfast
   To my daily desk I go :
First a fond salute bestowing
   On my Mary's ruby lips,
Which, perchance, may be rewarded
   With a pair of playful nips.

All day long across the ledger
   Still my patient pen I drive,
Thinking what a feast awaits me
   In my happy home at five ;
In my small one-storeyed Eden,
   Where my wife awaits my coming,
And our solitary handmaid
   Mutton-chops with care is crumbing.

When the clock proclaims my freedom,
   Then my hat I seize and vanish ;
Every trouble from my bosom,
   Every anxious care I banish.
Swiftly brushing o'er the pavement.
   At a furious pace I go,
Till I reach my darling dwelling
   In the wilds of Pimlico.

" Mary, wife, where art thou, dearest !"
   Thus I cry, while yet afar ;
Ah ! what scent invades my nostrils ?—
   'Tis the smoke of a cigar !
Instantly into the parlour
   Like a maniac I haste,
And I find a young Life-Guardsman,
   With his arm round Mary's waist.
And his other hand is playing
   Most familiarly with hers ;
And I think my Brussels carpet
   Somewhat damaged by his spurs.
" Fire and furies ! what the blazes ?"
   Thus in frenzied wrath I call ;
When my spouse her arms upraises,
   With a most astounding squall.
" Was there ever such a monster,
   Ever such a wretched wife !

— · ·

Ah! how long must I endure it,
    How protract this hateful life?
All day long, quite unprotected,
    Does he leave his wife at home:
And she cannot see her cousins,
    Even when they kindly come!"

Then the young Life-Guardsman, rising,
    Scarce vouchsafes a single word,
But, with look of deadly menace,
    Claps his hand upon his sword:
And in fear I faintly falter—
    "This your cousin, then he's mine!
Very glad, indeed, to see you,—
    Won't you stop with us, and dine?"

Won't a ferret suck a rabbit?—
    As a thing of course he stops;
And with most voracious swallow
    Walks into my mutton-chops.
In the twinkling of a bed-post
    Is each savoury platter clear,
And he shows uncommon science
    In his estimate of beer.

Half-and-half goes down before him.
    Gurgling from the pewter pot;

And he moves a counter motion
    For a glass of something hot.
Neither chops nor beer I grudge him,
    Nor a moderate share of goes ;
But I know not why he's always
    Treading upon Mary's toes.

Evermore, when, home returning,
    From the counting-house I come,
Do I find the young Life-Guardsman
    Smoking pipes and drinking rum.
Evermore he stays to dinner,
    Evermore devours my meal ;
For I have a wholesome horror
    Both of powder and of steel.

Yet I know he's Mary's cousin.
    For my only son and heir
Much resembles that young Guardsman,
    With the self-same curly hair ;
But I wish he would not always
    Spoil my carpet with his spurs ;
And I'd rather see his fingers
    In the fire, than touching hers.

The Queen in France.

PART I.

It fell upon the August month,
    When landsmen bide at hame,
That our gude Queen went out to sail
    Upon the saut-sea faem.

And she has ta'en the silk and gowd,
    The like was never seen ;

And she has ta'en the Prince Albert,
    And the bauld Lord Aberdeen.

" Ye'se bide at hame, Lord Wellington :
    Ye daurna gang wi' me :
For ye hae been ance in the land o' France.
    And that's eneuch for ye.

" Ye'se bide at hame, Sir Robert Peel,
    To gather the red and the white monie :
And see that my men dinna eat me up
    At Windsor wi' their gluttonie. "

They hadna sailed a league, a league,—
    A league, but barely twa,
When the lift grew dark, and the waves grew wan.
    And the wind began to blaw.

" O weel weel may the waters rise,
    In welcome o' their Queen ;
What gars ye look sae white, Albert ?
    What makes your ee sae green ? "

" My heart is sick, my heid is sair :
    Gie me a glass o' the gude brandie :
To set my foot on the braid green sward.
    I'd gie the half o' my yearly fee.

" It's sweet to hunt the sprightly hare
    On the bonny slopes o' Windsor lea,
But O, it's ill to bear the thud
    And pitching o' the saut saut sea ! "

And aye they sailed, and aye they sailed,
    Till England sank behind,
And over to the coast of France
    They drave before the wind.

Then up and spak the King o' France,
    Was birling at the wine ;
" O wha may be the gay ladye,
    That owns that ship sae fine ?

" And wha may be that bonny lad,
    That looks sae pale and wan ?
I'll wad my lands o' Picardie,
    That he's nae Englishman."

Then up and spak an auld French lord,
    Was sitting beneath his knee,
" It is the Queen o' braid England
    That's come across the sea."

" And O an it be England's Queen,
    She's welcome here the day ;
I'd rather hae her for a friend
    Than for a deadly fae.

"Gae, kill the cerock in the yard,
　　The auld sow in the sty,
And bake for her the brockit calf,
　　But and the puddock-pie!"

And he has gane until the ship,
　　As soon as it drew near,
And he has ta'en her by the hand—
　　"Ye're kindly welcome here!"

And syne he kissed her on ae cheek,
　　And syne upon the ither;
And he ca'd her his sister dear,
　　And she ca'd him her brither.

"Light doun, light doun now, ladye mine,
　　Light doun upon the shore;
Nae English king has trodden here
　　This thousand years and more."

"And gin I lighted on your land,
　　As light fu' weel I may,
O am I free to feast wi' you,
　　And free to come and gae?"

And he has sworn by the Haly Rood,
　　And the black stane o' Dumblane,
That she is free to come and gae
　　Till twenty days are gane.

" I've lippened to a Frenchman's aith,"
  Said gude Lord Aberdeen ;
" But I'll never lippen to it again
  Sae lang's the grass is green.

" Yet gae your ways, my sovereign liege,
  Sin' better mayna be ;
The wee bit bairns are safe at hame,
  By the blessing o' Marie !"

Then doun she lighted frae the ship.
  She lighted safe and sound ;
And glad was our good Prince Albert
  To step upon the ground.

" Is that your Queen, my Lord," she said.
  "That auld and buirdly dame ?
I see the crown upon her head ;
  But I dinna ken her name."

And she has kissed the Frenchman's Queen.
  And eke her daughters three,
And gien her hand to the young Princess.
  That louted upon the knee.

And she has gane to the proud castle.
  That's biggit beside the sea :
But aye, when she thought o' the bairns at hame.
  The tear was in her ee.

She gied the King the Cheshire cheese.
    But and the porter fine ;
And he gied her the puddock-pies,
    But and the blude-red wine.

Then up and spak the dourest Prince,
    An admiral was he ;
" Let's keep the Queen o' England here,
    Sin' better mayna be !

" O mony is the dainty king
    That we hae trappit here ;
And mony is the English yerl
    That's in our dungeons drear !"

" You lee, you lee, ye graceless loon,
    Sae loud's I hear ye lee !
There never yet was Englishman
    That came to skaith by me.

" Gae oot, gae oot, ye fause traitour !
    Gae oot until the street ;
It's shame that Kings and Queens should sit
    Wi' sic a knave at meat !"

Then up and raise the young French lord,
    In wrath and hie disdain—
" O ye may sit, and ye may eat
    Your puddock-pies alane !

" But were I in my ain gude ship,
     And sailing wi' the wind,
And did I meet wi' auld Napier,
     I'd tell him o' my mind."

O then the Queen leuch loud and lang,
     And her colour went and came :
"Gin ye meet wi' Charlie on the sea,
     Ye'd wish yersel at hame!"

And aye they birlit at the wine,
     And drank richt merrilie,
Till the auld cock crawed in the castle-yard,
     And the abbey bell struck three.

The Queen she gaed until her bed,
     And Prince Albert likewise ;
And the last word that gay ladye said
     Was—"O thae puddock-pies!"

PART II

The sun was high within the lift
     Afore the French King raise ;
And syne he louped intil his sark,
     And warslit on his claes.

"Gae up, gae up, my little foot-page,
　　Gae up until the toun ;
And gin ye meet wi' the auld harper,
　　Be sure ye bring him doun."

And he has met wi' the auld harper :
　　O but his een were reid ;
And the bizzing o' a swarm o' bees
　　Was singing in his heid.

" Alack ! alack !" the harper said,
　　" That this should e'er hae been ?
I daurna gang before my liege,
　　For I was fou yestreen."

" It's ye maun come, ye auld harper :
　　Ye daurna tarry lang ;
The King is just dementit-like
　　For wanting o' a sang."

And when he came to the King's chamber,
　　He loutit on his knee,
" O what may be your gracious will
　　Wi' an auld frail man like me ?"

" I want a sang, harper," he said,
　　" I want a sang richt speedilie :
And gin ye dinna make a sang,
　　I'll hang ye up on the gallows tree."

"I canna do't, my liege," he said,
    "Hae mercy on my auld grey hair!
But gin that I had got the words,
    I think that I might mak the air."

"And wha's to mak the words, fause loon,
    When minstrels we have barely twa:
And Lamartine is in Paris toun,
    And Victor Hugo far awa?"

"The deil may gang for Lamartine,
    And flee away wi' auld Hugo,
For a better minstrel than them baith
    Within this very toun I know.

"O kens my liege the gude Walter,
    At hame they ca' him BON GAULTIER?
He'll rhyme ony day wi' True Thomas,
    And he is in the castle here."

The French King first he lauchit loud,
    And syne did he begin to sing;
"My een are auld, and my heart is cauld,
    Or I suld hae known the minstrels' King.

"Gae take to him this ring o' gowd,
    And this mantle o' the silk sae fine,
And bid him mak a maister sang
    For his sovereign ladye's sake and mine."

"I winna take the gowden ring,
    Nor yet the mantle fine :.
But I'll mak the sang for my ladye's sake,
    And for a cup of wine."

The Queen was sitting at the cards,
    The King ahint her back ;
And aye she dealed the red honours,
    And aye she dealed the black :

And syne unto the dourest Prince
    She spak richt courteouslie ;—
"Now will ye play, Lord Admiral,
    Now will ye play wi' me ?"

The dourest Prince he bit his lip,
    And his brow was black as glaur :
"The only game that e'er I play
    Is the bluidy game o' war !"

"And gin ye play at that, young man,
    It weel may cost ye sair ;
Ye'd better stick to the game at cards,
    For you'll win nae honours there !"

The King he leuch, and the Queen she leuch,
    Till the tears ran blithely doun ;
But the Admiral he raved and swore,
    Till they kicked him frae the room.

The Harper came, and the Harper sang.
 And O but they were fain ;
For when he had sung the gude sang twice,
 They called for it again.

It was the sang o' the Field o' Gowd,
 In the days of auld langsyne ;
When bauld King Henry crossed the seas,
 Wi' his brither King to dine.

And aye he harped, and aye he carped,
 Till up the Queen she sprang—
" I'll wad a County Palatine,
 Gude Walter made that sang."

Three days had come, three days had gane,
 The fourth began to fa',
When our gude Queen to the Frenchman said,
 " It's time I was awa !

" O, bonny are the fields o' France,
 And saftly draps the rain ;
But my bairnies are in Windsor Tower,
 And greeting a' their lane.

" Now ye maun come to me, Sir King,
 As I have come to ye ;
And a benison upon your heid
 For a' your courtesie !

" Ye maun come, and bring your ladye fere ;
    Ye sall na say me no ;
And ye'se mind, we have aye a bed to spare
    For that gawsy chield Guizot."

Now he has ta'en her lily-white hand,
    And put it to his lip,
And he has ta'en her to the strand,
    And left her in her ship.

" Will ye come back, sweet bird," he cried,
    " Will ye come kindly here,
When the lift is blue, and the lavrocks sing,
    In the spring-time o' the year ? "

" It's I would blithely come, my Lord,
    To see ye in the spring ;
It's I would blithely venture back,
    But for ae little thing.

" It isna that the winds are rude,
    Or that the waters rise,
But I loe the roasted beef at hame,
    And no thae puddock-pies ! "

The Massacre of the Macpherson.

I.

FHAIRSHON swore a feud
    Against the clan M'Tavish :
Marched into their land
    To murder and to rafish :
For he did resolve
    To extirpate the vipers,
With four-and-twenty men
    And five-and-thirty pipers.

II.

But when he had gone
    Half-way down Strath Canaan,
Of his fighting tail
    Just three were remainin'.
They were all he had,
    To back him in ta battle ;
All the rest had gone
    Off, to drive ta cattle.

III.

" Fery coot!" cried Fhairshon,
    " So my clan disgraced is ;
Lads, we'll need to fight
    Pefore we touch the peasties.
Here's Mhic-Mac-Methusaleh
    Coming wi' his fassals,
Gillies seventy-three,
    And sixty Dhuinéwassails !"

IV.

" Coot tay to you, sir ;
    Are you not ta Fhairshon ?
Was you coming here
    To fisit any person ?

You are a plackguard, sir !
　　It is now six hundred
Coot long years, and more,
　　Since my glen was plundered."

V.

" Fat is tat you say ?
　　Dare you cock your peaver ?
I will teach you. sir.
　　Fat is coot pehaviour !
You shall not exist
　　For another day more :
I will shoot you, sir.
　　Or stap you with my claymore !"

VI.

" I am fery glad
　　To learn what you mention,
Since I can prevent
　　Any such intention."
So Mhic-Mac-Methusaleh
　　Gave some warlike howls.
Trew his skhian-dhu,
　　An' stuck it in his powels.

VII.

In this fery way
    Tied ta faliant Fhairshon,
Who was always thought
    A superior person.
Fhairshon had a son,
    Who married Noah's daughter,
And nearly spoiled ta Flood,
    By trinking up ta water:

VIII.

Which he would have done.
    I at least believe it.
Had ta mixture peen
    Only half Glenlivet.
This is all my tale :
    Sirs, I hope 'tis new t' ye !
Here's your fery good healths.
    And tamn ta whusky duty '

The Young Stockbroker's Bride.

"O SWIFTLY speed the gallant bark!—
    I say, you mind my luggage, porter!
I do not heed yon storm-cloud dark,
    I go to wed old Jenkin's daughter.
I go to claim my own Mariar,
    The fairest flower that blooms in Harwich
My panting bosom is on fire,
    And all is ready for the marriage."

Thus spoke young Mivins, as he stepped
   On board the " Firefly," Harwich packet :
The bell rung out, the paddles swept
   Plish-plashing round with noisy racket.
The lowering clouds young Mivins saw,
   But fear, he felt, was only folly ;
And so he smoked a fresh cigar,
   Then fell to whistling—" Nix my dolly !"

The wind it roared ; the packet's hulk
   Rocked with a most unpleasant motion :
Young Mivins leant him o'er a bulk,
   And poured his sorrows to the ocean.
Tints—blue and yellow—signs of woe—
   Flushed, rainbow-like, his noble face in,
As suddenly he rushed below,
   Crying, " Steward, steward, bring a basin !"

On sped the bark : the howling storm
   The funnel's tapering smoke did blow far :
Unmoved, young Mivins' lifeless form
   Was stretched upon a haircloth sofa.
All night he moaned, the steamer groaned,
   And he was hourly getting fainter ;
When it came bump against the pier,
   And there was fastened by the painter.

Young Mivins rose, arranged his clothes,
　　Caught wildly at his small portmanteau :
He was unfit to lie or sit,
　　And found it difficult to stand, too.
He sought the deck, he sought the shore,
　　He sought the lady's house like winking,
And asked, low tapping at the door,
　　" Is this the house of Mr Jenkin ?"

A short man came—he told his name—
　　Mivins was short—he cut him shorter,
For in a fury he exclaimed,
　　" Are you the man as vants my darter ?
Vot kim'd on you last night, young sqvire ?"
　　" It was the steamer, rot and scuttle her !"
" Mayhap it vos, but our Mariar
　　Valked off last night with Bill the butler.

" And so you've kim'd a post too late."
　　" It was the packet, sir, miscarried !"
" Vy, does you think a gal can vait
　　As sets 'er 'art on being married ?
Last night she vowed she'd be a bride,
　　And 'ave a spouse for vuss or better :
So Bill struck in ; the knot vos tied,
　　And now I vishes you may get her !"

Young Mivins turned him from the spot,
   Bewildered with the dreadful stroke, her
Perfidy came like a shot—
   He was a thunder-struck stockbroker.
" A curse on steam and steamers too !
   By their delays I have been undone !"
He cried, as, looking very blue,
   He rode a bachelor to London.

The Laureates' Tourney.

[This and the five following Poems were among those forwarded to the Home Secretary, by the unsuccessful competitors for the Laureateship, on its becoming vacant by the death of Southey. How they came into our possession is a matter between Sir James Graham and ourselves. The result of the contest could never have been doubtful, least of all to the great poet who then succeeded to the bays. His own sonnet on the subject is full of the serene consciousness of superiority, which does not even admit the idea of rivalry, far less of defeat.

Bays! which in former days have graced the brow
    Of some, who lived and loved, and sang and died;
    Leaves that were gathered on the pleasant side
Of old Parnassus from Apollo's bough;
With palpitating hand I take ye now,
    Since worthier minstrel there is none beside,
    And with a thrill of song half deified,
I bind them proudly on my locks of snow.
There shall they bide, till he who follows next,
    Of whom I cannot even guess the name,
Shall by Court favour, or some vain pretext
    Of fancied merit, desecrate the same,—
And think, perchance, he wears them quite as well
As the sole bard who sang of Peter Bell!]

FYTTE THE FIRST.

"WHAT news, what news, thou pilgrim grey, what news
        from southern land?
How fare the bold Conservatives, how is it with Ferrand?
How does the little Prince of Wales—how looks our lady
        Queen?
And tell me, is the monthly nurse once more at Windsor
        seen?"

" I bring no tidings from the Court, nor from St Stephen's
　　hall ;
I've heard the thundering tramp of horse, and the trum-
　　pet's battle-call :
And these old eyes have seen a fight, which England ne'er
　　hath seen,
Since fell King Richard sobbed his soul through blood on
　　Bosworth Green.

' He's dead, he's dead, the Laureate's dead !'　'Twas thus
　　the cry began,
And straightway every garret-roof gave up its minstrel
　　man ;
From Grub Street, and from Houndsditch, and from Far-
　　ringdon Within,
The poets all towards Whitehall poured on with eldritch
　　din.

Loud yelled they for Sir James the Graham : but sore
　　afraid was he ;
A hardy knight were he that might face such a minstrelsie.
'Now by St Giles of Netherby, my patron Saint, I
　　swear,
I'd rather by a thousand crowns Lord Palmerston were
　　here !—

'What is't ye seek, ye rebel knaves, what make you
        there beneath!'
'The bays, the bays! we want the bays! we seek the
        laureate wreath!
We seek the butt of generous wine that cheers the sons
        of song:
Choose thou among us all, Sir Knight—we may not tarry
        long!'

Loud laughed the good Sir James in scorn—'Rare jest it
        were, I think,
But one poor butt of Xeres, and a thousand rogues to
        drink!
An' if it flowed with wine or beer, 'tis easy to be
        seen,
That dry within the hour would be the well of Hippo-
        crene.

'Tell me, if on Parnassus' heights there grow a thousand
        sheaves:
Or has Apollo's laurel bush yet borne ten hundred
        leaves?
Or if so many leaves were there, how long would they
        sustain
The ravage and the glutton bite of such a locust train?

'No! get ye back into your dens, take counsel for the
    night,
And choose me out two champions to meet in deadly
    fight:
To-morrow's dawn shall see the lists marked out in Spital-
    fields,
And he who wins shall have the bays, and he shall die
    who yields!'

Down went the window with a crash,—in silence and in
    fear
Each ragged bard looked anxiously upon his neighbour
    near;
Then up and spake young Tennyson—'Who's here that
    fears for death?
'Twere better one of us should die, than England lose the
    wreath!

'Let's cast the lots among us now, which two shall fight
    to-morrow;—
For armour bright we'll club our mite, and horses we can
    borrow.
'Twere shame that bards of France should sneer, and
    German *Dichters* too,
If none of British song might dare a deed of *derring-do!*'

'The lists of Love are mine,' said Moore, 'and not the
  lists of Mars :'
Said Hunt. 'I seek the jars of wine, but shun the combat's jars !'
'I'm old,' quoth Samuel Rogers.—' Faith,' says Campbell, 'so am I !'
'And I'm in holy orders, sir !' quoth Tom of Ingoldsby.

'Now out upon ye, craven loons !' cried Moxon, good at
  need,—
'Bide, if ye will, secure at home, and sleep while others
  bleed.
I second Alfred's motion, boys,—let's try the chance of
  lot ;
And monks shall sing, and bells shall ring, for him that
  goes to pot.'

Eight hundred minstrels slunk away — two hundred
  stayed to draw,—
Now Heaven protect the daring wight that pulls the
  longest straw !
'Tis done ! 'tis done ! And who hath won ? Keep silence
  one and all,—
The first is William Wordsworth hight, the second Ned
  Fitzball !

FYTTE THE SECOND.

"Oh, bright and gay hath dawned the day on lordly Spital-
fields,—
How flash the rays with ardent blaze from polished helms
and shields !
On either side the chivalry of England throng the green,
And in the middle balcony appears our gracious Queen.

With iron fists, to keep the lists, two valiant knights appear,
The Marquis Hal of Waterford, and stout Sir Aubrey Vere.
'What ho ! there, herald, blow the trump ! Let's see who
comes to claim
The butt of golden Xeres, and the Laureate's honoured
name !'

That instant dashed into the lists, all armed from head to
heel,
On courser brown, with vizor down, a warrior sheathed in
steel ;
Then said our Queen—'Was ever seen so stout a knight
and tall ?
His name—his race ?'—'An't please your grace, it is the
brave Fitzball.

'Oft in the Melodrama line his prowess hath been
    shown,
And well throughout the Surrey side his thirst for blood
    is known.
But see, the other champion comes!'—Then rung the
    startled air
With shouts of 'Wordsworth, Wordsworth, ho! the bard
    of Rydal's there.'

And lo! upon a little steed, unmeet for such a course,
Appeared the honoured veteran; but weak seemed man
    and horse.
Then shook their ears the sapient peers,—'That joust
    will soon be done:
My Lord of Brougham, I'll back Fitzball, and give you
    two to one!'

'Done,' quoth the Brougham,—'And done with you!'
    'Now, Minstrels, are you ready?'
Exclaimed the Lord of Waterford,—'You'd better both
    sit steady.
Blow, trumpets, blow the note of charge! and forward to
    the fight!'
'Amen!' said good Sir Aubrey Vere; 'Saint Schism
    defend the right!'

As sweeps the blast against the mast when blows the
    furious squall,
So started at the trumpet's sound the terrible Fitzball ;
His lance he bore his breast before,—Saint George pro-
    tect the just !
Or Wordsworth's hoary head must roll along the shame-
    ful dust !

' Who threw that calthrop ? Seize the knave !' Alas !
    the deed is done ;
Down went the steed, and o'er his head flew bright
    Apollo's sun.
' Undo his helmet ! cut the lace ! pour water on his
    head !'
' It ain't no use at all, my lord ; 'cos vy ? the covey's
    dead !'

Above him stood the Rydal bard—his face was full of
    woe.
' Now there thou liest, stiff and stark, who never feared a
    foe :
A braver knight, or more renowned in tourney and in
    hall,
Ne'er brought the upper gallery down, than terrible Fitz-
    ball !'

They led our Wordsworth to the Queen—she crowned
    him with the bays,
And wished him many happy years, and many quarter-
    days :
And if you'd have the story told by abler lips than
    mine,
You've but to call at Rydal Mount, and taste the
    Laureate's wine !"

The Royal Banquet.

THE Queen she kept high festival in Windsor's lordly
    hall,
And round her sat the gartered knights, and ermined
    nobles all :
There drank the valiant Wellington, there fed the wary
    Peel,
And at the bottom of the board Prince Albert carved the
    veal.

" What, pantler, ho ! remove the cloth !   Ho ! cellarer,
    the wine,
And bid the royal nurse bring in the hope of Brunswick's
    line !"
Then rose with one tumultuous shout the band of British
    peers,
" God bless her sacred Majesty !   Let's see the little
    dears !"

Now by Saint George, our patron saint, 'twas a touching
    sight to see
That iron warrior gently place the Princess on his
    knee ;
To hear him hush her infant fears, and teach her how to
    gape
With rosy mouth expectant for the raisin and the
    grape !

They passed the wine, the sparkling wine—they filled the
    goblets up :
Even Brougham, the cynic anchorite, smiled blandly on
    the cup ;
And Lyndhurst, with a noble thirst, that nothing could
    appease,
Proposed the immortal memory of King William on his
    knees.

" What want we here, my gracious liege," cried gay Lord
    Aberdeen,
" Save gladsome song and minstrelsy to flow our cups
    between ?
I ask not now for Goulburn's voice or Knatchbull's
    warbling lay,
But where's the Poet Laureate to grace our board to-
    day !"

Loud laughed the Knight of Netherby, and scornfully he
    cried,
" Or art thou mad with wine, Lord Earl, or art thyself
    beside ?
Eight hundred Bedlam bards have claimed the Laureate's
    vacant crown,
And now like frantic Bacchanals run wild through London
    town !"

" Now glory to our gracious Queen !" a voice was heard
    to cry,
And dark Macaulay stood before them all with frenzied
    eye ;
" Now glory to our gracious Queen, and all her glorious
    race,
A boon, a boon, my sovran liege ! Give me the Laureate's
    place !

"'Twas I that sang the might of Rome, the glories of
    Navarre :
And who could swell the fame so well of Britain's Isles
    afar ?
The hero of a hundred fights—" Then Wellington up
    sprung,
"Ho, silence in the ranks, I say ! Sit down, and hold
    your tongue !

"By heaven, thou shalt not twist my name into a jingling
    lay,
Or mimic in thy puny song the thunders of Assaye !
'Tis hard that for thy lust of place in peace we cannot
    dine.
Nurse, take her Royal Highness, here ! Sir Robert, pass
    the wine !"

"No Laureate need we at our board !" then spoke the
    Lord of Vaux :
"Here's many a voice to charm the ear with minstrel
    song, I know.

Even I myself—" Then rose the cry- " A song, a song
 from Brougham !"
He sang,—and straightway found himself alone within
 the room.

The Bard of Erin's Lament.

Oh, weep for the hours, when the little blind boy
    Wove round me the spells of his Paphian bower ;
When I dipped my light wings in the nectar of joy,
    And soared in the sunshine, the moth of the hour !
From beauty to beauty I passed, like the wind ;
    Now fondled the lily, now toyed with the rose ;
And the fair, that at morn had enchanted my mind,
    Was forsook for another ere evening's close.

I sighed not for honour, I cared not for fame,
    While Pleasure sat by me, and Love was my guest :
They twined a fresh wreath for each day as it came,
    And the bosom of Beauty still pillowed my rest :
And the harp of my country—neglected it slept—
    In hall or by greenwood unheard were its songs ;
From Love's Sybarite dreams I aroused me, and swept
    Its chords to the tale of her glories and wrongs.

But weep for the hour!—Life's summer is past,
　　And the snow of its winter lies cold on my brow;
And my soul, as it shrinks from each stroke of the blast.
　　Cannot turn to a fire that glows inwardly now.
No, its ashes are dead—and, alas! Love or Song
　　No charm to Life's lengthening shadows can lend.
Like a cup of old wine, rich, mellow, and strong,
　　And a seat by the fire *tête-à-tête* with a friend.

The Laureate.

'Tis I would be the Laureate bold!
When the days are hot, and the sun is strong,
I'd lounge in the gateway all the day long,
With her Majesty's footmen in crimson and gold
I'd care not a pin for the waiting-lord;
But I'd lie on my back on the smooth greensward,
With a straw in my mouth, and an open vest,
And the cool wind blowing upon my breast,
And I'd vacantly stare at the clear blue sky,
And watch the clouds as listless as I.
          Lazily, lazily
And I'd pick the moss and daisies white,
And chew their stalks with a nibbling bite,
And I'd let my fancies roam abroad
In search of a hint for a birthday ode.
          Crazily, crazily

Oh, that would be the life for me,
With plenty to get and nothing to do,
But to deck a pet poodle with ribbons of blue,
And whistle all day to the Queen's cockatoo.
          Trance-somely, trance-somely
Then the chambermaids, that clean the rooms,
Would come to the windows and rest on their brooms,
With their saucy caps and their crispéd hair,
And they'd toss their heads in the fragrant air.

And say to each other—"Just look down there,
At the nice young man, so tidy and small,
Who is paid for writing on nothing at all,
            Handsomely, handsomely!"

They would pelt me with matches and sweet pastilles,
And crumpled-up balls of the royal bills,
Giggling and laughing, and screaming with fun,
As they'd see me start, with a leap and a run,
From the broad of my back to the points of my toes,
When a pellet of paper hit my nose,
            Teasingly, sneezingly.
Then I'd fling them bunches of garden flowers,
And hyacinths plucked from the Castle bowers :
And I'd challenge them all to come down to me,
And I'd kiss them all till they kissed me,
            Laughingly, laughingly.

Oh, would not that be a merry life,
Apart from care, and apart from strife,
With the Laureate's wine, and the Laureate's pay,
And no deductions at quarter-day !
Oh, that would be the post for me !

With plenty to get and nothing to do
But to deck a pet poodle with ribbons of blue,
And whistle a tune to the Queen's cockatoo,
And scribble of verses remarkably few,
And at evening empty a bottle or two,
　　　Quaffingly, quaffingly!

　　　'Tis I would be
　　　　　The Laureate bold,
　　　With my butt of sherry
　　　To keep me merry,
And nothing to do but to pocket my gold!

A Midnight Meditation.

FILL me once more the foaming pewter up!
  Another board of oysters, ladye mine!
To-night Lucullus with himself shall sup.
  These Mute inglorious Miltons are divine!
  And as I here in slippered ease recline,
Quaffing of Perkins's Entire my fill,
I sigh not for the lymph of Aganippe's rill.

A nobler inspiration fires my brain.
  Caught from Old England's fine time-hallowed drink:
I snatch the pot again, and yet again,
  And as the foaming fluids shrink and shrink,
  Fill me once more, I say, up to the brink!
This makes strong hearts—strong heads attest its charm—
This nerves the might that sleeps in Britain's brawny arm!

But these remarks are neither here nor there.
  Where was I? Oh, I see—old Southey's dead!
They'll want some bard to fill the vacant chair,
  And drain the annual butt—and oh, what head
  More fit with laurel to be garlanded

Than this, which, curled in many a fragrant coil,
Breathes of Castalia's streams, and best Macassar oil!

I know a grace is seated on my brow,
   Like young Apollo's with his golden beams--
There should Apollo's bays be budding now:—
    And in my flashing eyes the radiance beams
    That marks the poet in his waking dreams.
When, as his fancies cluster thick and thicker,
He feels the trance divine of poesy and liquor.

They throng around me now, those things of air,
   That from my fancy took their being's stamp:
There Pelham sits and twirls his glossy hair,
    There Clifford leads his pals upon the tramp:
    There pale Zanoni, bending o'er his lamp,
Roams through the starry wilderness of thought,
Where all is everything, and everything is nought.

Yes, I am he who sung how Aram won
   The gentle ear of pensive Madeline!
How love and murder hand in hand may run,
   Cemented by philosophy serene,
   And kisses bless the spot where gore has been!

Who breathed the melting sentiment of crime,
And for the assassin waked a sympathy sublime !

Yes, I am he, who on the novel shed
 Obscure philosophy's enchanting light !
Until the public, 'wildered as they read,
 Believed they saw that which was not in sight—
 Of course 'twas not for me to set them right :
For in my nether heart convinced I am,
Philosophy's as good as any other bam.

Novels three-volumed I shall write no more—
 Somehow or other now they will not sell :
And to invent new passions is a bore—
 I find the Magazines pay quite as well.
 Translating's simple, too, as I can tell,
Who've hawked at Schiller on his lyric throne,
And given the astonished bard a meaning all my own.

Moore, Campbell, Wordsworth, their best days are grassed ;
 Battered and broken are their early lyres.
Rogers, a pleasant memory of the past,
 Warmed his young hands at Smithfield's martyr fires,
 And, worth a plum, nor bays nor butt desires.
But these are things would suit me to the letter,
For though this Stout is good, old Sherry's greatly better.

A fico for your small poetic ravers,
    Your Hunts, your Tennysons, your Milnes, and these!
Shall they compete with him who wrote 'Maltravers,'
    Prologue to ' Alice or the Mysteries' !
    No ! Even now my glance prophetic sees
My own high brow girt with the bays about.
What ho ! within there, ho ! another pint of STOUT !

Stout !   *More Stout !!*

Montgomery.

A POEM.

LIKE one who, waking from a troublous dream,
Pursues with force his meditative theme :
Calm as the ocean in its halcyon still,
Calm as the sunlight sleeping on the hill :
Calm as at Ephesus great Paul was seen
To rend his robes in agonies serene ;
Calm as the love that radiant Luther bore
To all that lived behind him, and before :
Calm as meek Calvin, when, with holy smile,
He sang the mass around Servetus' pile,—
So once again I snatch this harp of mine,
To breathe rich incense from a mystic shrine.
Not now to whisper to the ambient air
The sounds of Satan's Universal Prayer :
Not now to sing, in sweet domestic strife
That woman reigns the Angel of our life :
But to proclaim the wish, with pious art,
Which thrills through Britain's universal heart,—
That on this brow, with native honours graced,
The Laureate's chaplet should at length be placed !

Fear not, ye maids, who love to hear me speak :
Let no desponding tears bedim your cheek !
No gust of envy, no malicious scorn,
Hath this poor heart of mine with frenzy torn.
There are who move so far above the great,
Their very look disarms the glance of hate ;
Their thoughts, more rich than emerald or gold,
Enwrap them like the prophet's mantle's fold.
Fear not for me, nor think that this our age,
Blind though it be, hath yet no Archimage.
I, who have bathed in bright Castalia's tide,
By classic Isis and more classic Clyde ;
I, who have handled, in my lofty strain,
All things divine, and many things profane ;
I, who have trod where seraphs fear to tread ;
I, who on mount——no, " honey-dew" have fed :
I, who undaunted broke the mystic seal,
And left no page for prophets to reveal ;
I, who in shade portentous Dante threw ;
I, who have done what Milton dared not do,—
I fear no rival for the vacant throne ;
No mortal thunder shall eclipse my own!

Let dark Macaulay chant his Roman lays,
Let Monckton Milnes go maunder for the bays,
Let Simmons call on great Napoleon's shade,
Let Lytton Bulwer seek his Aram's aid,

Let Wordsworth ask for help from Peter Bell,
Let Campbell carol Copenhagen's knell,
Let Delta warble through his Delphic groves,
Let Elliott shout for pork and penny loaves,—
I care not, I ! resolved to stand or fall ;
One down, another on, I'll smash them all !

Back, ye profane ! this hand alone hath power
To pluck the laurel from its sacred bower ;
This brow alone is privileged to wear
The ancient wreath o'er hyacinthine hair ;
These lips alone may quaff the sparkling wine,
And make its mortal juice once more divine.
Back, ye profane !   And thou, fair Queen, rejoice :
A nation's praise shall consecrate thy choice.
Thus, then, I kneel where Spenser knelt before,
On the same spot, perchance, of Windsor's floor ;
And take, while awe-struck millions round me stand,
The hallowed wreath from great Victoria's hand.

The Death of Space.

[Why has Satan's own Laureate never given to the world his marvellous threnody on "The Death of Space"? Who knows where the bays might have fallen, had he forwarded that mystic manuscript to the Home Office? If unwonted modesty withholds it from the public eye, the public will pardon the boldness that tears from blushing obscurity the following fragments of this unique poem.]

ETERNITY shall raise her funeral pile
    In the vast dungeon of the extinguished sky,
And, clothed in dim barbaric splendour, smile,
    And murmur shouts of elegiac joy.

While those that dwell beyond the realms of space,
    And those that people all that dreary void,
When old Time's endless heir hath run his race,
    Shall live for aye, enjoying and enjoyed.

And 'mid the agony of unsullied bliss,
    Her Demogorgon's doom shall Sin bewail,
The undying serpent at the spheres shall hiss,
    And lash the empyrean with his tail.

And Hell, inflated with supernal wrath,
    Shall open wide her thunder-bolted jaws,
And shout into the dull cold ear of Death,
    That he must pay his debt to Nature's laws.

And when the King of Terrors breathes his last,
    Infinity shall creep into her shell,
Cause and effect shall from their thrones be cast,
    And end their strife with suicidal yell :

While from their ashes, burnt with pomp of kings
    'Mid incense floating to the evanished skies,
Nonentity, on circumambient wings,
    An everlasting Phœnix shall arise.

Little John and the Red Friar.

A LAY OF SHERWOOD.

FYTTE THE FIRST.

THE deer may leap within the glade ;
    The fawns may follow free—
For Robin is dead, and his bones are laid
    Beneath the greenwood tree.

And broken are his merry, merry men,
    That goodly companie :
There's some have ta'en the northern road
    With Jem of Netherbee.

The best and bravest of the band
    With Derby Ned are gone ;
But Earlie Grey and Charlie Wood,
    They stayed with Little John.

Now Little John was an outlaw proud,
    A prouder ye never saw ;
Through Nottingham and Leicester shires
    He thought his word was law,
And he strutted through the greenwood wide,
    Like a pestilent jack-daw.

He swore that none, but with leave of him,
    Should set foot on the turf so free :
And he thought to spread his cutter's rule
    All over the south countrie.
" There's never a knave in the land," he said,
    " But shall pay his toll to me ! "

And Charlie Wood was a taxman good
    As ever stepped the ground,

He levied mail, like a sturdy thief,
From all the yeomen round.
"Nay, stand!" quoth he, "thou shalt pay to me
Seven pence from every pound!"

Now word has come to Little John,
As he lay upon the grass,
That a Friar red was in merry Sherwood
Without his leave to pass.

"Come hither, come hither, my little foot-page!
Ben Hawes, come tell to me,
What manner of man is this burly frere
Who walks the woods so free?"

"My master good!" the little page said,
"His name I wot not well,
But he wears on his head a hat so red,
With a monstrous scallop-shell.

"He says he is Prior of Copmanshurst,
And Bishop of London town,
And he comes with a rope from our father the Pope,
To put the outlaws down.

"I saw him ride but yester-tide
　　With his jolly chaplains three ;
And he swears that he has an open pass
　　From Jem of Netherbee !"

Little John has ta'en an arrow so broad,
　　And broke it o'er his knee ;
"Now may I never strike doe again,
　　But this wrong avenged shall be !

"And has he dared, this greasy frere,
　　To trespass in my bound,
Nor asked for leave from Little John
　　To range with hawk and hound ?

"And has he dared to take a pass
　　From Jem of Netherbee,
Forgetting that the Sherwood shaws
　　Pertain of right to me ?

"O were he but a simple man,
　　And not a slip-shod frere !
I'd hang him up by his own waist-rope
　　Above yon tangled brere.

"O did he come alone from Jem,
    And not from our father the Pope,
I'd bring him in to Copmanshurst,
    With the noose of a hempen rope !

" But since he has come from our father the Pope,
    And sailed across the sea,
And since he has power to bind and loose,
    His life is safe for me ;
But a heavy penance he shall do
    Beneath the greenwood tree !"

" O tarry yet !" quoth Charlie Wood,
    "O tarry, master mine !
It's ill to shear a yearling hog,
    Or twist the wool of swine !

" It's ill to make a bonny silk purse,
    From the ear of a bristly boar ;
It's ill to provoke a shaveling's curse,
    When the way lies him before.

" I've walked the forest for twenty years,
    In wet weather and dry,

And never stopped a good fellowe,
    Who had no coin to buy.

" What boots it to search a beggarman's bags,
    When no silver groat he has ?
So, master mine, I rede you well,
    E'en let the Friar pass !"

"Now cease thy prate," quoth Little John,
    " Thou japest but in vain ;
An he have not a groat within his pouch,
    We may find a silver chain.

" But were he as bare as a new-flayed buck,
    As truly he may be,
He shall not tread the Sherwood shaws
    Without the leave of me !"

Little John has taken his arrows and bow,
    His sword and buckler strong,
And lifted up his quarter-staff,
    Was full three cloth yards long.

And he has left his merry men
    At the trysting-tree behind,

And gone into the gay greenwood,
    This burly frere to find.

O'er holt and hill, through brake and brere,
    He took his way alone—
Now, Lordlings, list and you shall hear
    This geste of Little John.

FYTTE THE SECOND.

'Tis merry, 'tis merry in gay greenwood,
    When the little birds are singing,
When the buck is belling in the fern,
    And the hare from the thicket springing!

'Tis merry to hear the waters clear,
    As they splash in the pebbly fall;
And the ouzel whistling to his mate,
    As he lights on the stones so small.

But small pleasaunce took Little John
    In all he heard and saw;
Till he reached the cave of a hermit old
    Who wonned within the shaw.

"*Ora pro nobis!*" quoth Little John—
    His Latin was somewhat rude—
"Now. holy father, hast thou seen
    A frere within the wood?

"By his scarlet hose, and his ruddy nose,
    I guess you may know him well;
And he wears on his head a hat so red,
    And a monstrous scallop-shell."

"I have served Saint Pancras," the hermit said,
    "In this cell for thirty year,
Yet never saw I, in the forest bounds,
    The face of such a frere!

"And if ye find him, master mine,
    E'en take an old man's advice,
And raddle him well, till he roar again,
    Lest ye fail to meet him twice!"

"Trust me for that!" quoth Little John—
    "Trust me for that!" quoth he, with a laugh;
"There never was man of woman born,
    That asked twice for the taste of my quarter-
        staff!"

Then Little John he strutted on,
    Till he came to an open bound,
And he was aware of a Red Friar,
    Was sitting upon the ground.

His shoulders they were broad and strong,
    And large was he of limb;
Few yeomen in the north countrie
    Would care to mell with him.

He heard the rustling of the boughs,
    As Little John drew near;
But never a single word he spoke,
    Of welcome or of cheer;
Less stir he made than a pedlar would
    For a small gnat in his ear!

I like not his looks! thought Little John.
    Nor his staff of the oaken tree.
Now may our Lady be my help,
    Else beaten I well may be!

" What dost thou here, thou strong Friar,
    In Sherwood's merry round,
Without the leave of Little John,
    To range with hawk and hound !"

"Small thought have I," quoth the Red Friar.
    "Of any leave, I trow ;
That Little John is an outlawed thief,
    And so, I ween, art thou !

" Know, I am Prior of Copmanshurst,
    And Bishop of London town,
And I bring a rope from our father the Pope,
    To put the outlaws down."

Then out spoke Little John in wrath,
    " I tell thee, burly frere,
The Pope may do as he likes at home,
    But he sends no Bishops here !

" Up, and away, Red Friar !" he said,
    " Up, and away, right speedilie ;
An it were not for that cowl of thine,
    Avenged on thy body I would be !"

" Nay, heed not that," said the Red Friar,
    " And let my cowl no hindrance be ;
I warrant that I can give as good
    As ever I think to take from thee !"

Little John he raised his quarter-staff,
    And so did the burly priest,
And they fought beneath the greenwood tree,
    A stricken hour at least.

But Little John was weak of fence,
    And his strength began to fail ;
Whilst the Friar's blows came thundering down,
    Like the strokes of a threshing flail.

" Now hold thy hand, thou stalwart Friar,
    Now rest beneath the thorn,
Until I gather breath enow,
    For a blast at my bugle-horn !"

" I'll hold my hand," the Friar said,
    " Since that is your propine,
But, an you sound your bugle-horn,
    I'll even blow on mine !"

Little John he wound a blast so shrill
    That it rung o'er rock and linn,
And Charlie Wood and his merry men all
    Came lightly bounding in.

The Friar he wound a blast so strong
   That it shook both bush and tree,
And to his side came Witless Will,
   And Jem of Netherbee ;
With all the worst of Robin's band,
   And many a Rapparee !

Little John he wist not what to do,
   When he saw the others come ;
So he twisted his quarter-staff between
   His fingers and his thumb.

"There's some mistake, good Friar !" he said,
   "There's some mistake 'twixt thee and me ;
I know thou art Prior of Copmanshurst,
   But not beneath the greenwood tree.

"And if you will take some other name,
   You shall have ample leave to bide ;
With pasture also for your Bulls,
   And power to range the forest wide."

"There's no mistake !" the Friar said,
   "I'll call myself just what I please.
My doctrine is that chalk is chalk,
   And cheese is nothing else than cheese."

"So be it, then!" quoth Little John ;
    " But surely you will not object,
If I and all my merry men
    Should treat you with reserved respect !

" We can't call you Prior of Copmanshurst,
    Nor Bishop of London town,
Nor on the grass, as you chance to pass,
    Can we very well kneel down.

" But you'll send the Pope my compliments,
    And say, as a further hint,
That, within the Sherwood bounds, you saw
Little John, who is the son-in-law
    Of his friend, old Mat-o'-the-Mint!"

So ends this geste of Little John—
    God save our noble Queen!
But, Lordlings, say—Is Sherwood now
    What Sherwood once hath been?

The Rhyme of Sir Launcelot Bogle.

A LEGEND OF GLASGOW.

By Mrs ——— ——— ———

THERE's a pleasant place of rest, near a City of the West,
Where its bravest and its best find their grave.

Below the willows weep, and their hoary branches steep
    In the waters still and deep,
                        Not a wave !

And the old Cathedral Wall, so scathed and grey and
            tall,
    Like a priest surveying all, stands beyond :
And the ringing of its bell, when the ringers ring it
            well,
    Makes a kind of tidal swell
                        On the pond !

And there it was I lay, on a beauteous summer's day,
    With the odour of the hay floating by :
And I heard the blackbirds sing, and the bells demurely
            ring,
    Chime by chime, ting by ting,
                        Droppingly.

Then my thoughts went wandering back, on a very beaten
            track,
    To the confine deep and black of the tomb ;
And I wondered who he was, that is laid beneath the
            grass,
    Where the dandelion has
                        Such a bloom.

Then I straightway did espy, with my slantly-sloping eye,
  A carvèd stone hard by, somewhat worn ;
And I read in letters cold—𝔚𝔢𝔯𝔢. 𝔩𝔶𝔢𝔰. 𝔏𝔞𝔲𝔫𝔠𝔢𝔩𝔬𝔱. 𝔶𝔢. 𝔟𝔬𝔩𝔡𝔢.
  𝔒𝔣𝔣. 𝔶𝔢. 𝔯𝔞𝔠𝔢. 𝔬𝔣𝔣. 𝔅𝔬𝔤𝔦𝔩𝔢. 𝔬𝔩𝔡,
                𝔊𝔩𝔞𝔰𝔤𝔬𝔴. 𝔟𝔬𝔯𝔫𝔢.

𝔚𝔢. 𝔴𝔞𝔩𝔰. 𝔞𝔫𝔢. 𝔟𝔞𝔩𝔭𝔞𝔲𝔫𝔱. 𝔨𝔫𝔶𝔠𝔥𝔱𝔢. 𝔪𝔞𝔦𝔰𝔱. 𝔱𝔢𝔯𝔯𝔦𝔟𝔩𝔢. 𝔦𝔫. 𝔣𝔶𝔠𝔥𝔱𝔢.
  Here the letters failed outright, but I knew
That a stout crusading lord, who had crossed the Jordan's
          ford,
  Lay there beneath the sward,
                Wet with dew.

Time and tide they passed away, on that pleasant summer's
          day,
  And around me, as I lay, all grew old :
Sank the chimneys from the town, and the clouds of
          vapour brown
  No longer, like a crown,
                O'er it rolled.

Sank the great Saint Rollox stalk, like a pile of dingy chalk :
  Disappeared the cypress walk, and the flowers :
And a donjon keep arose, that might baffle any foes,
  With its men-at-arms in rows,
                On the towers.

And the flag that flaunted there showed the grim and
      grizzly bear,
   Which the Bogles always wear for their crest.
And I heard the warder call, as he stood upon the wall,
   "Wake ye up ! my comrades all,
                           From your rest !

"For, by the blessed rood, there's a glimpse of armour
      good
   In the deep Cowcaddens wood, o'er the stream ;
And I hear the stifled hum of a multitude that come,
   Though they have not beat the drum,
                           It would seem !

"Go tell it to my Lord, lest he wish to man the ford
   With partisan and sword, just beneath ;
Ho, Gilkison and Nares !   Ho, Provan of Cowlairs !
   We'll back the bonny bears
                           To the death !"

To the tower above the moat, like one who heedeth not,
   Came the bold Sir Launcelot, half undressed ;
On the outer rim he stood, and peered into the wood,
   With his arms across him glued
                           On his breast.

And he muttered, " Foe accurst ! hast thou dared to seek
　　me first ?
George of Gorbals, do thy worst—for I swear,
O'er thy gory corpse to ride, ere thy sister and my bride,
　　From my undissevered side
　　　　　　Thou shalt tear !

" Ho, herald mine, Brownlee ! ride forth, I pray, and see,
　　Who, what, and whence is he, foe or friend !
Sir Roderick Dalgleish, and my foster-brother Neish,
　　With his bloodhounds in the leash,
　　　　　　Shall attend."

Forth went the herald stout, o'er the drawbridge and
　　without,
　　Then a wild and savage shout rose amain,
Six arrows sped their force, and, a pale and bleeding corse.
　　He sank from off his horse
　　　　　　On the plain !

Back drew the bold Dalgleish, back started stalwart Neish,
　　With his bloodhounds in the leash, from Brownlee.
" Now shame be to the sword that made thee knight and
　　lord,
　　Thou caitiff thrice abhorred,
　　　　　　Shame on thee !

" Ho, bowmen, bend your bows!   Discharge upon the
        foes
    Forthwith no end of those heavy bolts.
Three angels to the brave who finds the foe a grave,
    And a gallows for the slave
                    Who revolts!"

Ten days the combat lasted : but the bold defenders
        fasted,
    While the foemen, better pastied, fed their host ;
You might hear the savage cheers of the hungry Gorbaliers,
    As at night they dressed the steers
                    For the roast.

And Sir Launcelot grew thin, and Provan's double chin
    Showed sundry folds of skin down beneath :
In silence and in grief found Gilkison relief,
    Nor did Neish the spell-word, beef,
                    Dare to breathe.

To the ramparts Edith came, that fair and youthful dame,
    With the rosy evening flame on her face.
She sighed, and looked around on the soldiers on the ground,
    Who but little penance found,
                    Saying grace !

And she said unto her lord, as he leaned upon his sword,
   "One short and little word may I speak?
I cannot bear to view those eyes so ghastly blue,
   Or mark the sallow hue
             Of thy cheek?

"I know the rage and wrath that my furious brother hath
   Is less against us both than at me.
Then, dearest, let me go, to find among the foe
   An arrow from the bow,
             Like Brownlee?"

"I would soil my father's name, I would lose my treasured
        fame,
   Ladye mine, should such a shame on me light:
While I wear a belted brand, together still we stand,
   Heart to heart, hand in hand!"
             Said the knight.

"All our chances are not lost, as your brother and his
        host
   Shall discover to their cost rather hard!
Ho, Provan! take this key—hoist up the Malvoisie,
   And heap it, d'ye see,
             In the yard.

" Of usquebaugh and rum, you will find, I reckon, some,
    Besides the beer and mum, extra stout ;
Go straightway to your tasks, and roll me all the casks,
    As also range the flasks,
                    Just without.

" If I know the Gorbaliers, they are sure to dip their ears
    In the very inmost tiers of the drink.
Let them win the outer court, and hold it for their sport,
    Since their time is rather short,
                    I should think !"

With a loud triumphant yell, as the heavy drawbridge fell,
    Rushed the Gorbaliers pell-mell, wild as Druids ;
Mad with thirst for human gore, how they threatened and
            they swore,
    Till they stumbled on the floor,
                    O'er the fluids !

Down their weapons then they threw, and each savage
            soldier drew
    From his belt an iron screw, in his fist ;
George of Gorbals found it vain their excitement to
            restrain,
    And indeed was rather fain
                    To assist.

With a beaker in his hand, in the midst he took his stand,
　　And silence did command, all below—
" Ho ! Launcelot the bold, ere thy lips are icy cold,
　　In the centre of thy hold,
　　　　　　　　Pledge me now !

" Art surly, brother mine ? In this cup of rosy wine,
　　I drink to the decline of thy race !
Thy proud career is done, thy sand is nearly run,
　　Never more shall setting sun
　　　　　　　　Gild thy face !

" The pilgrim, in amaze, shall see a goodly blaze,
　　Ere the pallid morning rays flicker up ;
And perchance he may espy certain corpses swinging
　　　　high !
　　What, brother ! art thou dry ?
　　　　　　　　Fill my cup !"

Dumb as death stood Launcelot, as though he heard him
　　　　not,
　　But his bosom Provan smote, and he swore :
And Sir Roderick Dalgleish remarked aside to Neish.
　　" Never sure did thirsty fish
　　　　　　　　Swallow more !

"Thirty casks are nearly done, yet the revel's scarce
    begun :
  It were knightly sport and fun to strike in !"
" Nay, tarry till they come," quoth Neish, " unto the
    rum—
  They are working at the mum.
              And the gin :"

Then straight there did appear to each gallant Gorbalier
  Twenty castles dancing near, all around ;
The solid earth did shake, and the stones beneath them
    quake,
  And sinuous as a snake
             Moved the ground.

Why and wherefore they had come, seemed intricate to
    some,
  But all agreed the rum was divine.
And they looked with bitter scorn on their leader highly
    born,
  Who preferred to fill his horn
             Up with wine !

Then said Launcelot the tall, " Bring the chargers from
    their stall ;
  Lead them straight unto the hall, down below :

Draw your weapons from your side, fling the gates asunder
        wide,
    And together we shall ride
                On the foe ! "

Then Provan knew full well, as he leaped into his selle,
    That few would 'scape to tell how they fared :
And Gilkison and Nares, both mounted on their mares,
    Looked terrible as bears,
                All prepared.

With his bloodhounds in the leash, stood the iron-sinewed
        Neish,
    And the falchion of Dalgleish glittered bright—
" Now, wake the trumpet's blast ; and, comrades, follow
        fast :
    Smite them down unto the last ! "
                Cried the knight.

In the cumbered yard without, there was shriek, and yell,
        and shout,
    As the warriors wheeled about, all in mail.
On the miserable kerne, fell the death-strokes stiff and stern,
    As the deer treads down the fern,
                In the vale !

Saint Mungo be my guide !   It was goodly in that tide
    To see the Bogle ride in his haste ;
He accompanied each blow with a cry of " Ha ! " or
            " Ho ! "
    And always cleft the foe
                    To the waist.

" George of Gorbals—craven lord ! thou didst threat me
            with the cord ;
    Come forth and brave my sword, if you dare ! "
But he met with no reply, and never could descry
    The glitter of his eye
                    Anywhere.

Ere the dawn of morning shone, all the Gorbaliers were
            down,
    Like a field of barley mown in the ear :
It had done a soldier good, to see how Provan stood,
    With Neish all bathed in blood,
                    Panting near.

" Now ply ye to your tasks—go carry down those casks,
    And place the empty flasks on the floor.
George of Gorbals scarce will come, with trumpet and
            with drum,
    To taste our beer and rum
                    Any more ! "

So they plied them to their tasks, and they carried down
    the casks,
  And replaced the empty flasks on the floor ;
But pallid for a week was the cellar-master's cheek,
  For he swore he heard a shriek
          Through the door.

When the merry Christmas came, and the Yule-log lent
    its flame
  To the face of squire and dame in the hall,
The cellarer went down to tap October brown,
  Which was rather of renown
          'Mongst them all.

He placed the spigot low, and gave the cask a blow,
  But his liquor would not flow through the pin.
" Sure, 'tis sweet as honeysuckles !" so he rapped it with
    his knuckles,
  But a sound, as if of buckles,
          Clashed within.

" Bring a hatchet, varlets, here !" and they cleft the cask
    of beer :
  What a spectacle of fear met their sight !
There George of Gorbals lay, skull and bones all blanched
    and grey,
  In the arms he bore the day
          Of the fight !

I have sung this ancient tale, not, I trust, without avail,
    Though the moral ye may fail to perceive :
Sir Launcelot is dust, and his gallant sword is rust,
    And now, I think, I must

                  Take my leave :

The Lay of the Lover's Friend.

[— H. ... ...]

I WOULD all womankind were dead,
    Or banished o'er the sea ;
For they have been a bitter plague
    These last six weeks to me :
It is not that I'm touched myself,
    For that I do not fear ;

No female face hath shown me grace
For many a bygone year,
But 'tis the most infernal bore,
Of all the bores I know,
To have a friend who's lost his heart
A short time ago.

Whene'er we steam it to Blackwall,
Or down to Greenwich run,
To quaff the pleasant cider-cup,
And feed on fish and fun :
Or climb the slopes of Richmond Hill,
To catch a breath of air :
Then, for my sins, he straight begins
To rave about his fair.
Oh, 'tis the most tremendous bore,
Of all the bores I know,
To have a friend who's lost his heart
A short time ago.

In vain you pour into his ear
Your own confiding grief :
In vain you claim his sympathy,
In vain you ask relief :
In vain you try to rouse him by
Joke, repartee, or quiz :

His sole reply's a burning sigh,
　　And " What a mind it is !"
　　　　O Lord ! it is the greatest bore,
　　　　　　Of all the bores I know,
　　　　　　To have a friend who's lost his heart
　　　　　　　A short time ago.

I've heard her thoroughly described
　　A hundred times, I'm sure ;
And all the while I've tried to smile,
　　And patiently endure ;
He waxes strong upon his pangs,
　　And potters o'er his grog ;
And still I say, in a playful way—
　　" Why, you're a lucky dog !"
　　　　But oh ! it is the heaviest bore,
　　　　　　Of all the bores I know,
　　　　　　To have a friend who's lost his heart
　　　　　　　A short time ago.

I really wish he'd do like me,
　　When I was young and strong :
I formed a passion every week,
　　But never kept it long.
But he has not the sportive mood
　　That always rescued me,

And so I would all women could
Be banished o'er the sea.
For 'tis the most egregious bore,
Of all the bores I know,
To have a friend who's lost his heart
A short time ago.

Francesca Da Rimini

TO BON GAULTIER.

[ARGUMENT.—An impassioned pupil of Leigh Hunt, having met Bon Gaultier at a Fancy Ball, declares the destructive consequences thus]

DIDST thou not praise me, Gaultier, at the ball,
Ripe lips, trim boddice, and a waist so small,
With clipsome lightness, dwindling ever less,
Beneath the robe of pea-y greeniness?
Dost thou remember, when, with stately prance,
Our heads went crosswise in the country dance:

How soft, warm fingers, tipped like buds of balm,
Trembled within the squeezing of thy palm ;
And how a cheek grew flushed and peachy-wise ·
At the frank lifting of thy cordial eyes ?
Ah, me ! that night there was one gentle thing,
Who, like a dove, with its scarce feathered wing,
Fluttered at the approach of thy quaint swaggering !

There's wont to be, at conscious times like these,
An affectation of a bright-eyed ease.—
A crispy cheekiness, if so I dare
Describe the swaling of a jaunty air ;
And thus, when swirling from the waltz's wheel,
You craved my hand to grace the next quadrille,
That smiling voice, although it made me start,
Boiled in the meek o'erlifting of my heart ;
And, picking at my flowers, I said, with free
And usual tone, "O yes, sir, certainly !"

Like one that swoons, 'twixt sweet amaze and fear,
I heard the music burning in my ear,
And felt I cared not, so thou wert with me,
If Gurth or Wamba were our vis-à-vis.
So, when a tall Knight Templar ringing came,
And took his place amongst us with his dame,
I neither turned away, nor bashful shrunk
From the stern survey of the soldier-monk.

Though rather more than three full quarters drunk ;
But, threading through the figure, first in rule,
I paused to see thee plunge into La Poule.

Ah, what a sight was that !   Not prurient Mars,
Pointing his toe through ten celestial bars—
Not young Apollo, beamily arrayed
In tripsome guise for Juno's masquerade—
Not smartest Hermes, with his pinion girth,
Jerking with freaks and snatches down to earth,
Looked half so bold, so beautiful, and strong,
As thou, when pranking through the glittering throng !
How the calmed ladies looked with eyes of love
On thy trim velvet doublet laced above :
The hem of gold, that, like a wavy river,
Flowed down into thy back with glancing shiver !
So bare was thy fine throat, and curls of black,
So lightsomely dropped in thy lordly back,
So crisply swaled the feather in thy bonnet,
So glanced thy thigh, and spanning palm upon it,
That my weak soul took instant flight to thee,
Lost in the fondest gush of that sweet witchery !

But when the dance was o'er, and arm in arm
(The full heart beating 'gainst the elbow warm)
We passed into the great refreshment-hall.
Where the heaped cheese-cakes and the comfits small

Lay, like a hive of sunbeams, brought to burn
Around the margin of the negus urn;
When my poor quivering hand you fingered twice,
And, with inquiring accents, whispered "Ice,
Water, or cream?" I could no more dissemble,
But dropped upon the couch all in a tremble.
A swimming faintness misted o'er my brain,
The corks seemed starting from the brisk champagne,
The custards fell untouched upon the floor,
Thine eyes met mine. That night we danced no more!

The Cadi's Daughter.

A LEGEND OF THE BOSPHORUS.

How beauteous is the star of night
    Within the eastern skies,
Like the twinkling glance of the Toorkman's lance,
    Or the antelope's azure eyes !
A lamp of love in the heaven above,
    That star is fondly streaming :
And the gay kiosk and the shadowy mosque
    In the Golden Horn are gleaming.

Young Leila sits in her jasmine bower,
   And she hears the bulbul sing,
As it thrills its throat to the first full note,
   That anthems the flowery spring.
She gazes still, as a maiden will,
   On that beauteous eastern star :
You might see the throb of her bosom's sob
   Beneath the white cymar !

She thinks of him who is far away,—
   Her own brave Galiongee,—
Where the billows foam and the breezes roam,
   On the wild Carpathian sea.
She thinks of the oath that bound them both
   Beside the stormy water ;
And the words of love, that in Athens' grove
   He spake to the Cadi's daughter.

" My Selim !" thus the maiden said,
   " Though severed thus we be,
By the raging deep and the mountains steep,
   My soul still yearns to thee.
Thy form so dear is mirrored here
   In my heart's pellucid well,
As the rose looks up to Phingari's orb,
   Or the moth to the gay gazelle.

" I think of the time when the Kaftan's crime
    Our love's young joys o'ertook,
And thy name still floats in the plaintive notes
    Of my silver-toned chibouque.
Thy hand is red with the blood it has shed,
    Thy soul it is heavy laden ;
Yet come, my Giaour, to thy Leila's bower ;
    Oh, come to thy Turkish maiden !"

A light step trod on the dewy sod,
    And a voice was in her ear,
And an arm embraced young Leila's waist-
    " Beloved ! I am here !"
Like the phantom form that rules the storm,
    Appeared the pirate lover,
And his fiery eye was like Zatanai,
    As he fondly bent above her.

" Speak, Leila, speak ; for my light caïque
    Rides proudly in yonder bay ;
I have come from my rest to her I love best,
    To carry thee, love, away.
The breast of thy lover shall shield thee, and cover
    My own jemscheed from harm ;
Think'st thou I fear the dark vizier,
    Or the mufti's vengeful arm ?

"Then droop not, love, nor turn away
    From this rude hand of mine!"
And Leila looked in her lover's eyes,
    And murmured—"I am thine!"
But a gloomy man with a yataghan
    Stole through the acacia blossoms,
And the thrust he made with his gleaming blade
    Hath pierced through both their bosoms.

"There! there! thou curséd caitiff Giaour!
    There, there, thou false one, lie!"
Remorseless Hassan stands above,
    And he smiles to see them die.
They sleep beneath the fresh green turf,
    The lover and the lady—
And the maidens wail to hear the tale
    Of the daughter of the Cadi!

The Dirge of the Drinker.

Brothers, spare awhile your liquor, lay your final tumbler
  down ;
He has dropped—that star of honour—on the field of his
  renown !
Raise the wail, but raise it softly, lowly bending on your
  knees,
If you find it more convenient, you may hiccup if you
  please.
Sons of Pantagruel, gently let your hip-hurraing sink,
Be your manly accents clouded, half with sorrow, half
  with drink !
Lightly to the sofa pillow lift his head from off the floor ;
See, how calm he sleeps, unconscious as the deadest nail
  in door !
Widely o'er the earth I've wandered ; where the drink
  most freely flowed,
I have ever reeled the foremost, foremost to the beaker
  strode.
Deep in shady Cider Cellars I have dreamed o'er heavy wet,
By the fountains of Damascus I have quaffed the rich
  sherbet,

Regal Montepulciano drained beneath its native rock,
On Johannis' sunny mountain frequent hiccuped o'er my
    hock ;
I have bathed in butts of Xeres deeper than did e'er Mon-
    soon,
Sangaree'd with bearded Tartars in the Mountains of the
    Moon :
In beer-swilling Copenhagen I have drunk your Danesman
    blind,
I have kept my feet in Jena, when each bursch to earth
    declined ;
Glass for glass, in fierce Jamaica, I have shared the planter's
    rum,
Drank with Highland dhuiné-wassails, till each gibbering
    Gael grew dumb :
But a stouter, bolder drinker—one that loved his liquor
    more—
Never yet did I encounter than our friend upon the floor !
Yet the best of us are mortal, we to weakness all are
    heir,
He has fallen, who rarely staggered—let the rest of us
    beware !
We shall leave him as we found him,—lying where his
    manhood fell,
'Mong the trophies of the revel, for he took his tipple well.
Better 'twere we loosed his neckcloth, laid his throat and
    bosom bare,

Pulled his Hobies off, and turned his toes to taste the
    breezy air.
Throw the sofa-cover o'er him, dim the flaring of the gas,
Calmly, calmly let him slumber, and, as by the bar we
    pass,
We shall bid that thoughtful waiter place beside him, near
    and handy,
Large supplies of soda-water, tumblers bottomed well with
    brandy.
So, when waking, he shall drain them, with that deathless
    thirst of his,—
Clinging to the hand that smote him, like a good 'un as
    he is !

The Death of Duval.

[" Methinks I see him already in the cart, sweeter and more lovely than the
nosegay in his hand! I hear the crowd extolling his resolution and intre-
pidity ! What volleys of sighs are sent from the windows of Holborn, that so
comely a youth should be brought to disgrace ! I see him at the tree ! the
whole circle are in tears ! even butchers weep !"—BEGGARS' OPERA.]

A LIVING sea of eager human faces,
 A thousand bosoms, throbbing all as one,
Walls, windows, balconies, all sorts of places,
 Holding their crowds of gazers to the sun :
 Through the hushed groups low-buzzing murmurs run ;
And on the air, with slow reluctant swell,
Comes the dull funeral boom of old Sepulchre's bell.

Oh, joy in London now ! in festal measure
 Be spent the evening of this festive day !
For thee is opening now a high-strung pleasure :
 Now, even now, in yonder press-yard they
 Strike from his limbs the fetters loose away !
A little while, and he, the brave Duval,
Will issue forth, serene, to glad and greet you all.

" Why comes he not ? say, wherefore doth he tarry ? "
    Starts the inquiry loud from every tongue.
"Surely," they cry, " that tedious Ordinary
    His tedious psalms must long ere this have sung,—
    Tedious to him that's waiting to be hung ! "
But hark ! old Newgate's doors fly wide apart.
" He comes, he comes ! "   A thrill shoots through each
    gazer's heart.

Joined in the stunning cry ten thousand voices,
    All Smithfield answered to the loud acclaim.
" He comes, he comes ! " and every breast rejoices,
    As down Snow Hill the shout tumultuous came,
    Bearing to Holborn's crowd the welcome fame.
" He comes, he comes ! " and each holds back his breath—
Some ribs are broke, and some few scores are crushed to
    death.

With step majestic to the cart advances
    The dauntless Claude, and springs into his seat.
He feels that on him now are fixed the glances
    Of many a Briton bold and maiden sweet,
    Whose hearts responsive to his glories beat.
In him the honour of " The Road " is centred,
And all the hero's fire into his bosom entered.

O

His was the transport—his the exultation
    Of Rome's great generals, when from afar,
Up to the Capitol, in the ovation,
    They bore with them, in the triumphal car,
    Rich gold and gems, the spoils of foreign war.
Io Triumphe ! They forgot their clay.
E'en so Duval, who rode in glory on his way.

His laced cravat, his kids of purest yellow.
    The many-tinted nosegay in his hand,
His large black eyes, so fiery, yet so mellow,
    Like the old vintages of Spanish land,
    Locks clustering o'er a brow of high command,
Subdue all hearts ; and, as up Holborn's steep
Toils the slow car of death, e'en cruel butchers weep.

He saw it, but he heeded not. His story,
    He knew, was graven on the page of Time.
Tyburn to him was as a field of glory,
    Where he must stoop to death his head sublime.
    Hymned in full many an elegiac rhyme.
He left his deeds behind him, and his name—
For he, like Cæsar, had lived long enough for fame.

He quailed not, save when, as he raised the chalice,—
    St Giles's bowl,—filled with the mildest ale,

To pledge the crowd, on her—his beauteous Alice—
  His eye alighted, and his cheek grew pale.
    She, whose sweet breath was like the spicy gale,
She, whom he fondly deemed his own dear girl,
Stood with a tall dragoon, drinking long draughts of
    purl.

He bit his lip—it quivered but a moment—
  Then passed his hand across his flushing brows :
He could have spared so forcible a comment
  Upon the constancy of woman's vows.
    One short sharp pang his hero-soul allows ;
But in the bowl he drowned the stinging pain,
And on his pilgrim course went calmly forth again.

A princely group of England's noble daughters
  Stood in a balcony suffused with grief,
Diffusing fragrance round them, of strong waters,
  And waving many a snowy handkerchief,
    Then glowed the prince of highwayman and thief !
His soul was touched with a seraphic gleam—
That woman could be false was but a mocking dream.

And now, his bright career of triumph ended,
  His chariot stood beneath the triple tree.
The law's grim finisher to its boughs ascended,

And fixed the hempen bandages, while he
Bowed to the throng, then bade the car go free.
The car rolled on, and left him dangling there,
Like famed Mohammed's tomb, uphung midway in air.

As droops the cup of the surcharged lily
    Beneath the buffets of the surly storm,
On the soft petals of the daffodilly,
    When Sirius is uncomfortably warm,
    So drooped his head upon his manly form,
While floated in the breeze his tresses brown.
He hung the stated time, and then they cut him down.

With soft and tender care the trainbands bore him,
    Just as they found him, nightcap, robe, and all,
And placed this neat though plain inscription o'er him,
    Among the atomics in Surgeons' Hall :
    "THESE ARE THE BONES OF THE RENOWNED DUVAL!"
There still they tell us, from their glassy case,
He was the last, the best of all that noble race !

Eastern Serenade.

THE minarets wave on the plain of Stamboul,
And the breeze of the evening blows freshly and cool;
The voice of the musnud is heard from the west,
And kaftan and kalpac have gone to their rest.
The notes of the kislar re-echo no more,
And the waves of Al Sirat fall light on the shore.

Where art thou, my beauty; where art thou, my bride?
Oh, come and repose by thy dragoman's side!

I wait for thee still by the flowery tophaik—
I have broken my Eblis for Zuleima's sake.
But the heart that adores thee is faithful and true,
Though it beats 'neath the folds of a Greek Allah-hu !

Oh, wake thee, my dearest ! the muftis are still,
And the tschocadars sleep on the Franguestan hill ;
No sullen aleikoum—no derveesh is here,
And the mosques are all watching by lonely Kashmere !
Oh, come in the gush of thy beauty so full,
I have waited for thee, my adored attar-gul !

I see thee—I hear thee—thy antelope foot
Treads lightly and soft on the velvet cheroot ;
The jewelled amaun of thy zemzem is bare,
And the folds of thy palampore wave in the air.
Come, rest on the bosom that loves thee so well,
My dove ! my phingari ! my gentle gazelle !

Nay, tremble not, dearest ! I feel thy heart throb,
'Neath the sheltering shroud of thy snowy kiebaub ;
Lo, there shines Muezzin, the beautiful star !
Thy lover is with thee, and danger afar :
Say, is it the glance of the haughty vizier,
Or the bark of the distant effendi, you fear !

Oh, swift fly the hours in the garden of bliss !
And sweeter than balm of Gehenna thy kiss !
Wherever I wander—wherever I roam,
My spirit flies back to its beautiful home ;
It dwells by the lake of the limpid Stamboul,
With thee, my adored one ! my own attar-gul !

Dame Fredegonde.

When folks, with headstrong passion blind.
To play the fool make up their mind,
They're sure to come with phrases nice,
And modest air, for your advice.
But as a truth unfailing make it,
They ask, but never mean to take it.
'Tis not advice they want, in fact,
But confirmation in their act.
Now mark what did, in such a case,
A worthy priest who knew the race.

A dame more buxom, blithe, and free,
Than Fredegonde you scarce would see.
So smart her dress, so trim her shape,
Ne'er hostess offered juice of grape;

Could for her trade wish better sign :
Her looks gave flavour to her wine,
And each guest feels it, as he sips,
Smack of the ruby of her lips.
A smile for all, a welcome glad,—
A jovial coaxing way she had :
And,—what was more her fate than blame,—
A nine months' widow was our dame.
But toil was hard, for trade was good,
And gallants sometimes will be rude.
" And what can a lone woman do ?
The nights are long, and eerie too.
Now, Guillot there's a likely man,
None better draws or taps a can :
He's just the man, I think, to suit,
If I could bring my courage to't."
With thoughts like these her mind is crossed :
The dame, they say, who doubts, is lost.
"But then the risk ?   I'll beg a slice
Of Father Raulin's good advice."

Prankt in her best, with looks demure,
She seeks the priest : and, to be sure,
Asks if he thinks she ought to wed :
" With such a business on my head,

I'm worried off my legs with care.
And need some help to keep things square.
I've thought of Guillot, truth to tell!
He's steady, knows his business well.
What do you think!"   When thus he met her:
"Oh, take him, dear, you can't do better!"
"But then the danger, my good pastor,
If the man I make the master.
There is no trusting to these men."
"Well, well, my dear, don't have him, then!"
"But help I must have: there's the curse.
I may go farther and fare worse."
"Why, take him, then!"   "But if he should
Turn out a thankless ne'er-do-good—
In drink and riot waste my all,
And rout me out of house and hall?"
"Don't have him, then!   But I've a plan
To clear your doubts, if any can.
The bells a peal are ringing.—hark!
Go straight, and what they tell you mark.
If they say 'Yes!' wed, and be blest—
If 'No,' why—do as you think best."

The bells rung out a triple bob:
Oh, how our widow's heart did throb,

As thus she heard their burden go.
" Marry, mar-marry, mar-Guillot !"
Bells were not then left to hang idle :
A week,—and they rang for her bridal.
But, woe the while, they might as well
Have rung the poor dame's parting knell.
The rosy dimples left her cheek,
She lost her beauties plump and sleek ;
For Guillot oftener kicked than kissed,
And backed his orders with his fist,
Proving by deeds as well as words.
That servants make the worst of lords.

She seeks the priest, her ire to wreak,
And speaks as angry women speak.
With tiger looks, and bosom swelling,
Cursing the hour she took his telling.
To all, his calm reply was this,—
" I fear you've read the bells amiss :
If they have led you wrong in aught,
Your wish, not they, inspired the thought.
Just go, and mark well what they say."
Off trudged the dame upon her way,
And sure enough their chime went so,—
" Don't have that knave, that knave Guillot !"

"Too true," she cried, "there's not a doubt :
What could my ears have been about?"
She had forgot, that, as fools think,
The bell is ever sure to clink.

The Death of Ishmael.

[This and the six following poems are examples of that new achievement of modern song—which, blending the *utile* with the *dulce*, symbolises at once the practical and spiritual characteristics of the age,—and is called familiarly " the puff poetical."]

DIED the Jew ?   " The Hebrew died.
   On the pavement cold he lay,
Around him closed the living tide ;
   The butcher's cad set down his tray :
The pot-boy from the Dragon Green
   No longer for his pewter calls ;
The Nereid rushes in between,
   Nor more her ' Fine live mackerel !' bawls."

Died the Jew ?   " The Hebrew died.
   They raised him gently from the stone,
They flung his coat and neckcloth wide—
   But linen had that Hebrew none.
They raised the pile of hats that pressed
   His noble head, his locks of snow ;
But, ah, that head, upon his breast,
   Sank down with an expiring ' Clo !' "

Died the Jew?   "The Hebrew died,
   Struck with overwhelming qualms
From the flavour spreading wide
   Of some fine Virginia Hams.
Would you know the fatal spot,
   Fatal to that child of sin?
These fine-flavoured hams are bought
   AT 50 BISHOPSGATE WITHIN!"

Parr's Life Pills.

'Twas in the town of Lubeck,
    A hundred years ago,
An old man walked into the church,
    With beard as white as snow :
Yet were his cheeks not wrinkled,
    Nor dim his eagle eye :
There's many a knight that steps the street,
Might wonder, should he chance to meet
    That man erect and high !

When silenced was the organ,
    And hushed the vespers loud,
The Sacristan approached the sire,
    And drew him from the crowd—
"There's something in thy visage,
    On which I dare not look ;
And when I rang the passing bell,
A tremor that I may not tell,
    My very vitals shook.

" Who art thou, awful stranger ?
    Our ancient annals say,
That twice two hundred years ago
    Another passed this way,

Like thee in face and feature :
   And, if the tale be true,
'Tis writ, that in this very year
Again the stranger shall appear.
   Art thou the Wandering Jew !"

"The Wandering Jew, thou dotard !"
   The wondrous phantom cried—
"'Tis several centuries ago
   Since that poor stripling died.
He would not use my nostrums—
   See, shaveling, here they are !
These put to flight all human ills,
These conquer death—unfailing pills,
   And I'm the inventor, PARR !"

Tarquin and the Augur.

GINGERLY is good King Tarquin shaving,
    Gently glides the razor o'er his chin,
Near him stands a grim Haruspex raving,
    And with nasal whine he pitches in
        Church extension hints,
        Till the monarch squints,
Snicks his chin, and swears—a deadly sin !

"Jove confound thee, thou bare-legged impostor !
    From my dressing-table get thee gone !
Dost thou think my flesh is double Glo'ster ?
    There again ! That cut was to the bone !
        Get ye from my sight ;
        I'll believe you're right
When my razor cuts the sharping hone !"

Thus spoke Tarquin with a deal of dryness :
    But the Augur, eager for his fees,
Answered—"Try it, your Imperial Highness :
    Press a little harder, if you please.

There ! the deed is done ! "
Through the solid stone
Went the steel as glibly as through cheese.

So the Augur touched the tin of Tarquin,
  Who suspected some celestial aid :
But he wronged the blameless gods ; for hearken !
  Ere the monarch's bet was rashly laid,
    With his searching eye
    Did the priest espy
Rogers' name engraved upon the blade.

La Mort d'Arthur.

NO. BY ALFRED TENNYS.

SLOWLY, as one who bears a mortal hurt,
Through which the fountain of his life runs dry.
Crept good King Arthur down unto the lake.
A roughening wind was bringing in the waves
With cold dull plash and plunging to the shore.
And a great bank of clouds came sailing up
Athwart the aspect of the gibbous moon,
Leaving no glimpse save starlight, as he sank,
With a short stagger, senseless on the stones.

No man yet knows how long he lay in swound :
But long enough it was to let the rust
Lick half the surface of his polished shield :
For it was made by far inferior hands,
Than forged his helm, his breastplate, and his greaves.
Whereon no canker lighted, for they bore
The magic stamp of MECHI'S SILVER STEEL.

Jupiter and the Indian Ale.

"Take away this clammy nectar!"
    Said the king of gods and men;
" Never at Olympus' table
    Let that trash be served again.
Ho, Lyæus, thou, the beery!
    Quick—invent some other drink;
Or, in a brace of shakes, thou standest
    On Cocytus' sulphury brink!"

Terror shook the limbs of Bacchus,
    Paly grew his pimpled nose,

And already in his rearward
    Felt he Jove's tremendous toes ;
When a bright idea struck him—
    " Dash my thyrsus ! I'll be bail—
For you never were in India—
    That you know not Hodgson's Ale ! "

" Bring it ! " quoth the Cloud-compeller ;
    And the wine-god brought the beer-
" Port and claret are like water
    To the noble stuff that's here ! "
And Saturnius drank and nodded,
    Winking with his lightning eyes,
And amidst the constellations
    Did the star of Hodgson rise !

The Lay of the Doudney Brothers.

Coats at five-and-forty shillings! trousers ten-and-six a
    pair!

Summer waistcoats, three a sov'reign, light and comfort-
    able wear!

Taglionis, black or coloured, Chesterfield and velveteen!

The old English shooting-jacket—doeskins, such as ne'er
    were seen!

Army cloaks and riding-habits, Alberts at a trifling cost!

Do you want an annual contract? Write to Doudneys'
    by the post.

Doudney Brothers! Doudney Brothers! Not the men
    that drive the van,

Plastered o'er with advertisements, heralding some paltry
    plan.

How, by base mechanic stinting, and by pinching of their
    backs,

Slim attorneys' clerks may manage to retrieve their
    Income-tax:

But the old established business—where the best of clothes
    are given

At the very lowest prices—Fleet Street, Number Ninety-
    seven.

Wouldst thou know the works of DOUDNEY? Hie thee
    to the thronged Arcade,
To the Park upon a Sunday, to the terrible Parade.
There, amid the bayonets bristling, and the flashing of the
    steel,
When the household troops in squadrons round the bold
    field-marshals wheel,
Shouldst thou see an aged warrior in a plain blue morning
    frock,
Peering at the proud battalions o'er the margin of his
    stock,—
Should thy throbbing heart then tell thee, that the veteran
    worn and grey
Curbed the course of Bonaparte, rolled the thunders of
    Assaye—
Let it tell thee, stranger, likewise, that the goodly garb
    he wears
Started into shape and being from the DOUDNEY BROTHERS'
    shears!
Seek thou next the rooms of Willis — mark, where
    D'Orsay's Count is bending,
See the trouser's undulation from his graceful hip
    descending;
Hath the earth another trouser so compact and love-
    compelling?
Thou canst find it, stranger, only, if thou seek'st the
    DOUDNEYS' dwelling!

Hark, from Windsor's royal palace, what sweet voice
     enchants the ear?

"Goodness, what a lovely waistcoat!   Oh, who made it,
     Albert dear?

'Tis the very prettiest pattern!   You must get a dozen
     others!"

And the Prince, in rapture, answers—"'Tis the work of
     DOUDNEY BROTHERS!"

Paris and Helen.

As the youthful Paris presses
    Helen to his ivory breast,
Sporting with her golden tresses,
    Close and ever closer pressed,

" Let me," said he, "quaff the nectar.
    Which thy lips of ruby yield :
Glory I can leave to Hector,
    Gathered in the tented field.

" Let me ever gaze upon thee.
    Look into thine eyes so deep :
With a daring hand I won thee,
    With a faithful heart I'll keep.

"Oh, my Helen, thou bright wonder.
    Who was ever like to thee ?
Jove would lay aside his thunder,
    So he might be blest like me.

" How mine eyes so fondly linger
    On thy soft and pearly skin :
Scan each round and rosy finger,
    Drinking draughts of beauty in !

" Tell me, whence thy beauty, fairest ?
    Whence thy cheek's enchanting bloom ?
Whence the rosy hue thou wearest,
    Breathing round thee rich perfume ? "

Thus he spoke, with heart that panted,
    Clasped her fondly to his side,
Gazed on her with look enchanted,
    While his Helen thus replied :

" Be no discord, love, between us,
    If I not the secret tell !
'Twas a gift I had of Venus,—
    Venus, who hath loved me well.

" And she told me as she gave it,
    ' Let not e'er the charm be known :
O'er thy person freely lave it,
    Only when thou art alone.'

" 'Tis enclosed in yonder casket—
    Here behold its golden key ;
But its name—love, do not ask it,
    Tell't I may not, even to thee : "

Long with vow and kiss he plied her :
  Still the secret did she keep,
Till at length he sank beside her,
  Seemed as he had dropped to sleep.

Soon was Helen laid in slumber,
  When her Paris, rising slow,
Did his fair neck disencumber
  From her rounded arms of snow.

Then, her heedless fingers oping,
  Takes the key and steals away,
To the ebon table groping,
  Where the wondrous casket lay :

Eagerly the lid uncloses,
  Sees within it, laid aslope,
PEARS' LIQUID BLOOM OF ROSES,
  Cakes of his TRANSPARENT SOAP !

Song of the Ennuyé.

I'm weary, and sick, and disgusted
    With Britain's mechanical din :
Where I'm much too well known to be trusted,
    And plaguily pestered for tin :
Where love has two eyes for your banker,
    And one chilly glance for yourself :
Where souls can afford to be franker,
    But when they're well garnished with pelf.

I'm sick of the whole race of poets,
    Emasculate, misty, and fine :
They brew their small-beer, and don't know its
    Distinction from full-bodied wine.
I'm sick of the prosers, that house up
    At drowsy St Stephen's,—ain't you?
I want some strong spirits to rouse up
    A good revolution or two!

I'm sick of a land, where each morrow
    Repeats the dull tale of to-day,
Where you can't even find a new sorrow
    To chase your stale pleasures away.
I'm sick of blue-stockings horrific,
    Steam, railroads, gas, scrip, and consols :
So I'll off where the golden Pacific
    Round islands of Paradise rolls.

There the passions shall revel unfettered,
    And the heart never speak but in truth,
And the intellect, wholly unlettered,
    Be bright with the freedom of youth ;
There the earth can rejoice in her blossoms,
    Unsullied by vapour or soot,
And there chimpanzees and opossums
    Shall playfully pelt me with fruit.

There I'll sit with my dark Orianas,
    In groves by the murmuring sea,
And they'll give, as I suck the bananas,
    Their kisses, nor ask them from me.
They'll never torment me for sonnets,
    Nor bore me to death with their own :
They'll ask not for shawls nor for bonnets,
    For milliners there are unknown.

There my couch shall be earth's freshest flowers,
    My curtains the night and the stars,
And my spirit shall gather new powers,
    Uncramped by conventional bars.
Love for love, truth for truth ever giving,
    My days shall be manfully sped;
I shall know that I'm loved while I'm living,
    And be wept by fond eyes when I'm dead!

Caroline.

LIGHTSOME, brightsome, cousin mine,
    Easy, breezy Caroline!
With thy locks all raven-shaded,
From thy merry brow up-braided,
And thine eyes of laughter full,
    Brightsome cousin mine!
Thou in chains of love hast bound me—
Wherefore dost thou flit around me,
    Laughter-loving Caroline?

When I fain would go to sleep
    In my easy-chair,
Wherefore on my slumbers creep—
Wherefore start me from repose,
Tickling of my hookèd nose,
    Pulling of my hair?
Wherefore, then, if thou dost love me,
So to words of anger move we,
    Corking of this face of mine,
    Tricksy cousin Caroline!

When a sudden sound I hear,
Much my nervous system suffers,
    Shaking through and through.
Cousin Caroline, I fear,
    'Twas no other, now, but you,
Put gunpowder in the snuffers,
    Springing such a mine!
Yes, it was your tricksy self,
Wicked-trickèd little elf,
    Naughty cousin Caroline!

Pins she sticks into my shoulder.
    Places needles in my chair,
And, when I begin to scold her,
    Tosses back her combèd hair.
    With so saucy-vexed an air,
That the pitying beholder
Cannot brook that I should scold her:
Then again she comes, and bolder,
    Blacks anew this face of mine,
    Artful cousin Caroline!

Would she only say she'd love me,
    Winsome tinsome Caroline,
Unto such excess 'twould move me.
    Teasing, pleasing, cousin mine!

That she might the live-long day
Undermine the snuffer-tray,
Tickle still my hookèd nose,
Startle me from calm repose
    With her pretty persecution ;
Throw the tongs against my shins,
Run me through and through with pins,
    Like a piercèd cushion ;
Would she only say she'd love me,
Darning-needles should not move me ;
But, reclining back, I'd say,
" Dearest ! there's the snuffer-tray ;
Pinch, O pinch those legs of mine !
Cork me, cousin Caroline ! "

To a Forget-Me-Not.

FOUND IN MY EMPORIUM OF LOVE-TOKENS.

Sweet flower, that with thy soft blue eye
    Didst once look up in shady spot,
To whisper to the passer-by
    Those tender words—Forget-me-not !

Though withered now, thou art to me
    The minister of gentle thought.—
And I could weep to gaze on thee,
    Love's faded pledge—Forget-me-not !

Thou speak'st of hours when I was young,
    And happiness arose unsought ;
When she, the whispering woods among,
    Gave me thy bloom - Forget-me-not !

That rapturous hour with that dear maid
    From memory's page no time shall blot.
When, yielding to my kiss, she said,
    "Oh, Theodore—Forget-me-not !"

Alas for love ! alas for truth !
    Alas for man's uncertain lot !
Alas for all the hopes of youth
    That fade like thee—Forget-me-not !

Alas for that one image fair,
    With all my brightest dreams inwrought !
That walks beside me everywhere,
    Still whispering—Forget-me-not !

Oh, Memory ! thou art but a sigh
    For friendships dead and loves forgot,
And many a cold and altered eye
    That once did say—Forget-me-not !

And I must bow me to thy laws,
    For—odd although it may be thought—
I can't tell who the deuce it was
    That gave me this Forget-me-not !

The Mishap.

" Why art thou weeping, sister ?
　　Why is thy cheek so pale ?
Look up, dear Jane, and tell me
　　What is it thou dost ail ?

" I know thy will is froward,
　　Thy feelings warm and keen,
And that *that* Augustus Howard
　　For weeks has not been seen.

" I know how much you loved him ;
    But I know thou dost not weep
For him ;—for though his passion be,
    His purse is noways deep.

" Then tell me why those tear-drops !
    What means this woeful mood !
Say, has the tax-collector
    Been calling, and been rude !

" Or has that hateful grocer,
    The slave ! been here to-day ?
Of course he had, by morrow's noon,
    A heavy bill to pay ?

" Come, on thy brother's bosom
    Unburden all thy woes :
Look up, look up, sweet sister ;
    Nay, sob not through thy nose."

" Oh, John, 'tis not the grocer
    For his account ; although
How ever he is to be paid,
    I really do not know.

" 'Tis not the tax-collector ;
    Though by his fell command
They've seized our old paternal clock,
    And new umbrella-stand !

" Nor that Augustus Howard,
    Whom I despise almost,—
But the soot's come down the chimney, John,
    And fairly spoiled the roast !"

Comfort in Affliction.

" WHEREFORE starts my bosom's lord !
    Why this anguish in thine eye !
Oh, it seems as thy heart's chord
    Had broken with that sigh !

" Rest thee, my dear lord, I pray,
    Rest thee on my bosom now !
And let me wipe the dews away,
    Are gathering on thy brow.

" There, again ! that fevered start !
    What, love ! husband ! is thy pain !
There is a sorrow on thy heart,
    A weight upon thy brain !

" Nay, nay, that sickly smile can ne'er
    Deceive affection's searching eye ;
'Tis a wife's duty, love, to share
    Her husband's agony.

"Since the dawn began to peep,
    Have I lain with stilled breath :
Heard thee moaning in thy sleep,
    As thou wert at grips with death.

"Oh, what joy it was to see
    My gentle lord once more awake !
Tell me, what is amiss with thee ?
    Speak, or my heart will break !"

"Mary, thou angel of my life,
    Thou ever good and kind ;
'Tis not, believe me, my dear wife,
    The anguish of the mind !

"It is not in my bosom, dear,
    No, nor my brain, in sooth :
But Mary, oh, I feel it here,
    Here in my wisdom tooth !

"Then give, — oh, first best antidote, —
    Sweet partner of my bed !
Give me thy flannel petticoat
    To wrap around my head !"

The Invocation.

" Brother, thou art very weary,
    And thine eye is sunk and dim.
And thy neckcloth's tie is crumpled,
    And thy collar out of trim :
There is dust upon thy visage,—
    Think not, Charles, I would hurt ye,
When I say, that altogether
    You appear extremely dirty.

" Frown not, brother, now, but hie thee
    To thy chamber's distant room :
Drown the odours of the ledger
    With the lavender's perfume.
Brush the mud from off thy trousers,
    O'er the china basin kneel,
Lave thy brows in water softened
    With the soap of Old Castile.

" Smooth the locks that o'er thy forehead
    Now in loose disorder stray ;
Pare thy nails, and from thy whiskers
    Cut those ragged points away ;

Let no more thy calculations
  Thy bewildered brain beset :
Life has other hopes than Cocker's,
  Other joys than tare and tret.

" Haste thee, for I ordered dinner,
  Waiting to the very last,
Twenty minutes after seven,
  And 'tis now the quarter past.
'Tis a dinner which Lucullus
  Would have wept with joy to see,
One, might wake the soul of Curtis
  From death's drowsy atrophy.

" There is soup of real turtle,
  Turbot, and the dainty sole :
And the mottled row of lobsters
  Blushes through the butter-bowl.
There the lordly haunch of mutton,
  Tender as the mountain grass,
Waits to mix its ruddy juices
  With the girdling caper-sauce.

" There a stag, whose branching forehead
  Spoke him monarch of the herds,
He whose flight was o'er the heather
  Swift as through the air the bird's,

Yields for thee a dish of cutlets ;
    And the haunch that wont to dash
O'er the roaring mountain-torrent,
    Smokes in most delicious hash.

"There, besides, are amber jellies
    Floating like a golden dream :
Ginger from the far Bermudas,
    Dishes of Italian cream :
And a princely apple-dumpling,
    Which my own fair fingers wrought,
Shall unfold its nectared treasures
    To thy lips all smoking hot.

" Ha ! I see thy brow is clearing,
    Lustre flashes from thine eyes :
To thy lips I see the moisture
    Of anticipation rise.
Hark ! the dinner-bell is sounding !"
    "Only wait one moment, Jane :
I'll be dressed, and down, before you
    Can get up the iced champagne !"

The Husband's Petition.

COME hither, my heart's darling.
　　Come, sit upon my knee,
And listen, while I whisper
　　A boon I ask of thee.
You need not pull my whiskers
　　So amorously, my dove ;
'Tis something quite apart from
　　The gentle cares of love.

I feel a bitter craving—
　　A dark and deep desire,
That glows beneath my bosom
　　Like coals of kindled fire.
The passion of the nightingale,
　　When singing to the rose,

THE HUSBAND'S PETITION.

Is feebler than the agony
    That murders my repose !

Nay, dearest ! do not doubt me,
    Though madly thus I speak
I feel thy arms about me,
    Thy tresses on my cheek :
I know the sweet devotion
    That links thy heart with mine,—
I know my soul's emotion
    Is doubly felt by thine :

And deem not that a shadow
    Hath fallen across my love :
No, sweet, my love is shadowless,
    As yonder heaven above.
These little taper fingers—
    Ah, Jane ! how white they be !—
Can well supply the cruel want
    That almost maddens me.

Thou wilt not sure deny me
    My first and fond request :
I pray thee, by the memory
    Of all we cherish best—
By all the dear remembrance
    Of those delicious days,
When, hand in hand, we wandered
    Along the summer braes :

By all we felt, unspoken,
    When 'neath the early moon,
We sat beside the rivulet,
    In the leafy month of June:
And by the broken whisper
    That fell upon my ear,
More sweet than angel music,
    When first I wooed thee, dear!

By thy great vow which bound thee
    For ever to my side,
And by the ring that made thee
    My darling and my bride!
Thou wilt not fail nor falter,
    But bend thee to the task—
A BOILED SHEEP'S-HEAD ON SUNDAY
    Is all the boon I ask!

Sonnet to Britain.

Halt! Shoulder arms! Recover!
    As you were!
Right wheel! Eyes left! Attention!
    Stand at ease!
O Britain! O my country! Words like these
    Have made thy name a terror and a fear
To all the nations. Witness Ebro's banks,
    Assaye, Toulouse, Nivelle, and Waterloo,
    Where the grim despot muttered—*Sauve qui peut!*
And Ney fled darkling.—Silence in the ranks!

Inspired by these, amidst the iron crash
　　Of armies, in the centre of his troop
The soldier stands—unmovable, not rash—
　　Until the forces of the foeman droop ;
Then knocks the Frenchmen to eternal smash,
　　Pounding them into mummy.　Shoulder, hoop !

THE END

In Small Quarto, printed on Toned Paper, bound in gilt cloth, 21s.,

AYTOUN'S
LAYS OF THE SCOTTISH CAVALIERS,

ILLUSTRATED BY

J. NOEL PATON and W. H. PATON, A.R.S.A.

Engraved by John Thompson, W. J. Linton, W. Thomas, Whymper,
Cooper, Green, Dalziels, Evans, &c.

OPINIONS OF THE PRESS.

Standard.

The artists have excelled themselves in the engravings which they have
furnished. Seizing the spirit of Mr Aytoun's 'Ballads,' as, perhaps, none but
Scotchmen could have seized it, they have thrown their whole strength into
the work with a heartiness which others would do well to imitate. Whoever
there may be that does not already know these 'Lays,' we recommend at once
to make their acquaintance in this edition, wherein author and artist illustrate
each other as kindred spirits should.

Daily Review.

Of all our illustrated books there has been none so magnificent as this.
. . . . . This is a beautiful book. There was never a Christmas book like
it ; and we lay it down with a reluctance which is not the most common
feeling of the reviewer.

Saturday Review.

This is, on the whole, one of the very best of the Christmas books, and
certainly one which puts forth high artistic claims.

Illustrated London News.

This is, to look upon, a kingly, a lordly, and a knightly book : it has an
outer dress worthy of the kings and lords and knights whose deeds are the
theme of the spirited strains imprinted on its pages. The illustrations, too,
which adorn the pages, full well deserve the handsome covers which preserve
them, as it were, in a costly casket. They are gems of art wrought by skilful
artificers—by J. Noel Paton and Waller H. Paton. The former is mighty in
the delineation of figures, the latter graceful in landscape scenery.

The Bookseller.

Sometimes it has been a difficult matter to decide which book was entitled
to the prize ; fortunately, this year the task is easy one volume being so
considerably raised above its fellows by the exquisite beauty and elaborate
finish of the drawings, worthily seconded by the labours of the engravers,
themselves artists, that the first place will readily be conceded to this edition
of Aytoun's 'Lays of the Scottish Cavaliers.'

LATELY PUBLISHED.

THE ODES OF HORACE. Translated by Theodore Martin.
With Life and Notes. Second Edition. Post 8vo, 9s.

CATULLUS. Translated into English Verse by the Same.
With Life and Notes. Post 8vo, 6s. 6d.

THE VITA NUOVA OF DANTE. Translated by the Same.
With an Introduction and Notes. Square 8vo, 7s. 6d.

ALADDIN: A Dramatic Poem. By Adam Oehlenschlaeger.
Translated by the Same. Fcap. 8vo, 5s.

CORREGGIO: A Tragedy. By Oehlenschlaeger. Translated
by the Same. With Notes. Fcap. 8vo, 2s. 6d.

KING RENE'S DAUGHTER: A Danish Lyrical Drama.
Translated by the Same. Square 8vo, 2s. 6d.

POEMS AND BALLADS OF GOETHE. Translated by
W. EDMONDSTOUNE AYTOUN, D.C.L., and THEODORE MAR-
TIN. Second Edition. In foolscap 8vo, 6s.

BOTHWELL: A Poem. By W. Edmondstoune Aytoun, D.C.L.,
Author of ' Lays of the Scottish Cavaliers,' &c. Third Edition, fcap.
8vo, 7s. 6d.

THE BALLADS OF SCOTLAND. Edited by W. Edmond-
STOUNE AYTOUN, D.C.L. Second Edition, Two Vols. fcap., 12s.

FIRMILIAN; or, **THE STUDENT OF BADAJOZ.** A
SPASMODIC TRAGEDY. By T. PERCY JONES. Elegantly
printed in small 8vo, 5s.

WILLIAM BLACKWOOD & SONS, EDINBURGH AND LONDON.

www.ingramcontent.com/pod-product-compliance
Lightning Source LLC
Chambersburg PA
CBHW020354030726
47496CB00007B/2137